Local Speed

Susan Pepper Robbins

For Oliver, Courtney, Remi, Thomas and Lulu

Contents

ONE

June 15

DEAD AND GONE......is what I'm calling this book.

To me, these words are beautiful even if the facts behind them are not. These words try to close a door on terrible things, although it is very hard to close a door in your life so that you can take the next breath and then the next one and your heart can slow down.

The basic truth about a closed door is that it does not keep terrible things behind it. They get out like smoke and mix in with the ordinary things.

Some smoke is white because it comes from wood burning. Some is black because it comes from old tires and oil burning. And not the new kind of smoke from the meth houses around here. I think the smoke that comes from under the door in my life is mostly gray. It would not be true to say that the smoke is black or that my life is terrible except for parts which are.

Still, it is good to try to close a door.

Lee Ann's teeth getting knocked out was an accident. How could it be my fault? I was saving Lee Ann, was what I was doing—not saving her in the way Uncle David needed saving in the river last summer. Lee Ann was not drowning—that's what Uncle David knew how to do and did perfectly.

I'll be glad to call my part in Lee Ann's accident any other name in the world. I am not stuck on the word "saving" the way I am on my favorite words—Dead and Gone.

Saving sounds a little too much like church or like what did not happen to Uncle David at the river as Mama stood over him holding her arms spread out to keep people away from him. She kept crying "Wait, Wait, Wait. Sometimes they come back from water. I've read about it. Sometimes they come back from drowning."

Of course, Uncle David did not come back, and Mama had to step back and let the rescue squad carry him away, not to the hospital, but straight to the funeral home.

Rescue Squad personnel have the authority to declare a person dead. They do not need a doctor to sign the paper. Mama says that is not right because rescue people might be wrong.

Maybe I was not saving my sister's life, but what would it be called when Keith Peller was trying to get Lee Ann to do things that were not right. Things that will get Lee Ann taken away from us if anyone knew about what he was up to, and get her put in another home where I will not be around to watch out for her. Not to mention the rape that is always in the corner of that man's mind, as a possibility if everything else he's trying fails. Not to mention the fact that a girl like Lee Ann can get pregnant. That sounds stupid but it's not.

If she is taken away from us, who will brush her hair and make the French braid down her back? Who will help her shave her legs and put lotion on them so that they gleam in the dark? If she leaves us! No one, that's who. So, she better stay put with me. I can keep her

3

away from Keith Peller. I am much smarter than he is. About a hundred times smarter as Mama says she is than everyone else in the world and then adds "for all the good it does me."

"Alcohol consumption" and maybe what would pass (with stupid people) for "abusive relationships" are what I had been worried about getting us in trouble with Family Services who would take Lee Ann away from us, but compared to what Keith Peller was getting ready to do to Lee Ann if he could get her (and me) into his van and take us somewhere, down one of the many roads around here where no one drives but people looking for good deals on local speed, alcohol and abuse are nothing to worry about.

Around here, we are known for our drugs which is, I guess, better than not being known at all. We make the newspaper every few months and always with the same angle on us as a problem: Who would think such a place would harbor criminals! Experts agree that the new drug market is hitting children just entering middle school and younger. Or as Ms. Karney says—I will explain who she is in a minute—"research suggests" that there is no formula for what makes a place like Sandys Point, population 336, the perfect place for "open-air drug markets."

We have our high bluffs along the river, good lookout points, and we have our places to tie up boats all along the banks. Kids in my class get paid to spot new comers, to sit in deer stands and watch for certain cars and ATV's coming in. They have lists of okay vehicles and not okay ones. They draw a line down a page between customers and nobodies, sometimes under the words "money" and "no money." I have seen the thrown away lists on crumpled notebook paper. The bad thing about kids is that they are not careful and leave signs everywhere. At night, very late, the Mercedes and Navigators line up around certain long driveways.

But it's really the grown people who are the greatest asset to a drug economy. Adults are reluctant, to say the least, to turn other people in, and most people around here anyway are reluctant to help the government. Kids, of course, won't turn anyone in. They know better. Because, for one thing, kids are easier to kill, a fact that is not lost on them, and for another, kids do not want to rat on anyone, even dealers. Even the white bread preppies at school have worked in the business. In fact, they are the best. Who suspects kids with plastic? They wear their nice shirts with the holes obviously cut in them and music in their ears to help pass the time as they check off their lists of known customers or clients, as they call them.

It is true that my family knows a lot about drugs, but in the old sense. The old, traditional drugs. Walter, not my real dad, married to Mama for ten years now, drinks sometimes, and yes, he drinks a lot sometimes. He is a classic binge drinker, not a sipper like Keith Peller who keeps a buzz on all the time.

Last summer I saw the beer cans rolling around in the back of Keith Peller's van, not old cans either, but all new ones. He would sweep them out in the ditches and then the floor of the van would fill up again as regular as the tides.

It's also true that there is a fair amount of yelling and screaming around here between Walter and Mama. Friendly fire. Nothing too serious, not what I think of as abusive, just loud, but someone who did not know us might take the noise for something bad. What Mama yells is worth writing down. Her favorite thing to say lately is what I wrote down earlier, "The trouble is that I'm about one hundred times as smart as anyone I know, for all the good it does me." She means it too, but it makes her sad to think she's all alone in the world seeing things so clearly, so it is not the same as being stuck on herself for being smarter than the world. She means she is smart enough to see what has happened to her—just about everything—and to look at it head on, eyeball to eyeball.

Ms. Karney does not understand the first thing about family life, an ignorance which is exactly why, Walter says, she got the job with Family Services of advising families and reporting them to authorities and ruining their lives.

Keith Peller is a serious problem, but Ms. Karney has no dreaming idea about him. After what happened with Lee Ann two weeks ago, or I should say, what did not happen, I see him everywhere, not just in my mind at night when I am in bed and ready to fall asleep. That's when I'd expect for a nightmare to begin. No, he doesn't wait for night. He comes in my head when he gets ready and stops my heart for five minutes or makes it jump around like a fish on a hook. I do not mean he's here in the flesh like he was here that afternoon two weeks ago in our room, as if he had every right to be there.

6

That's when I opened my eyes and there he was, standing, or rather crouching over Lee Ann, who was as usual, asleep, looking like Sleeping Beauty, awkward and beautiful just like Disney made her, trusting the world that she would wake up and do something fun and nice with me.

I know that I must make myself think about Keith Peller so that I get used to him and cannot be surprised or scared by him when he really does show up.

I must not close the door in my mind on his terrible face that's always half-smiling because he is not dead, much less gone, by a long shot. Oh no, he's here when he wants to be.

But he has not been here in our room, not in the flesh, not again since two weeks ago when he got in our room somehow without me hearing him. I can't believe it myself. But I was not listening for him or anyone. I was perfectly relaxed. Asleep.

But then, I opened my eyes, and there he was, tossing that stupid blonde hair out of his eyes.

I have made a plan for what I will do if he shows up again—in the flesh—though I do not think he will be crazy enough to try it again (the key word here is crazy, so he may) after hearing Lee Ann falling down the steps and Walter waking up. He knows that he could have ended up dead (and gone) if Walter had seen him. If he had found him in the house, found him upstairs in Lee Ann's and my room! And, if Mama had found him, he would have wished he were dead. Death would be the least of his problems, the best option.

Walter would have killed him with his bare hands. Easy. That's what he would have done as a first step. Walter knows how to kill from his marine training. Maybe murder would have been the best thing that could have happened. Then we would visit Walter in his cell at the State Farm. Murderers get out in a few years, especially the ones who kill people they know.

We can see the prison lights from here at night and they are pretty and soft because the State Farm is only forty miles away, and as I said, we are high above other places out here and can see across the state if we want to which we don't.

If Sandys Point were in Texas instead of here in Virginia, we would stare until we broke our eyes, but what is there to see in Virginia—the country part, anyway—but old houses, some fixed up, but most of them, like this one, left the way history intended: in ruins. I am quoting Mama on this point, but I agree.

My plan to avert an attempted rape the next time Keith Peller shows up is this: I will begin whisper-screaming that Lee Ann is HIV positive from her last visit to the hospital. I may have to scream out loud, and if Walter is at home set off the murder that would happen in the next few minutes. The HIV scare may not work because he probably has AIDS himself and wants to go around giving it to as many people as he can.

We are talking evil, folks. That's what Angela Marks, my best friend, would say and has said. "That man is evil personified," she says and goes on to expand on that brilliant idea, "but evil as a concept and evil in the flesh are two different kettles of fish."

Angela's vocabulary is very good and she loves ideas when she is the one who is expressing them.

Anyway, evil is tricky. It looks ordinary and familiar.

We are lucky that Keith Peller is evil as a concept most of the time, not in the flesh and not in the house and not in our bedroom.

As far as alcohol problems go—which seem simple compared to Keith Peller—show me a home in America without some alcohol consumption in it, and I'll report that home to Oprah who will do a show on "The Dry Home." Of course, I know there are dry homes; my point is that they are few and far between. There is always, in my experience, an old drunk uncle or aunt or a young cousin killing someone in a car or working off a DUI or going to rehab. No family is without its drunk in my opinion.

The drinking and yelling this family does are not worth mentioning. Recreational.

Two weeks ago: Keith Peller all of a sudden is standing here. Upstairs in Lee Ann's and my room breaking the rule that Walter thinks is the most important one in the world but he intends for children: don't roam around in other people's houses (or businesses, or countries). Grownups do not, as a usual thing, roam inside a house, but Walter knows that to kids, a house is unexplored territory, a neighboring planet handing out free tickets.

Walter hates to see children "set themselves on" a house, he calls it. He is talking from experience. When Uncle David's boys were here they knew every drawer, every closet, and Walter said he could feel them in his tool box, in his medicine cabinet, in his socks "for god's sake." This roaming rule is his only rule, but he applies it to everything.

I know I love a fresh house. I do. Walter says roaming's much worse than stealing because it's as if a thief came to look at everything you owned but didn't like anything, so he left everything different from the way he found it, so you end up insulted. It's more like an invasion that was only halfway successful because the soldiers decided they did not like the conquered territory and turned around and went home after messing with stuff.

I am careful when I roam. I do not scare people or wake them up or explore in a way that could pass for breaking and entering. Walter would never think of making a rule about grown-ups in houses. It would not occur to him or to Mama (they are forty-two and forty-one). Their old-fashioned assumption that grown-ups do not roam around in other people's homes is exactly how Keith Peller was able to get in this house with a lot more on his mind than roaming.

Keith Peller is counting on the fact that no one has even thought of a grown person being in a house, upstairs. Can you imagine saying, "Wait a minute, do not come into our home unless invited. Do not go into our daughters' room, especially through an upstairs window." Can you imagine even thinking such a thought? So, because of this vacuum in our heads, in Keith Peller sneaks.

And so, as I just said, Keith Peller appeared, a thief in the night, Mama calls him, only it was afternoon and she certainly did not know he was here and does not know it now. Lee Ann and I were dead asleep, thinking we were as safe as sand on the ocean floor, as a can of beans on the grocery store shelf.

When we open our eyes, he's sitting on Lee Ann's bed, so she can't get out, she's against the wall where she likes to wedge herself and he's on the side of the bed next to the door. He starts out by asking her if she doesn't want a shampoo. Of all things! A nice shampoo. He had himself a beauty salon, he said, over in Lynchburg, so he could do her.

This was the first I had heard about the salon, and who knows if it's true. It could be. We just know him as a motel maintenance man, painter and electrician, who attached himself to Uncle David and before we knew it, his girlfriend, Jeannine Turner, who always was with him, had married Uncle David! This was last summer.

I will write about that terrible wedding and the pre-wedding, something we had never heard of, later. At the wedding, everyone was crying up a storm, and there was a real storm with lightning and thunder. We all had to run but got soaked, Jeannine's mascara ran down her face and her hair flattened down, but it was too late to call off the wedding because Uncle David didn't seem to see her, the way she really looked. The storm should have told Uncle David that he was making a big mistake.

But yes, Keith Peller asks Lee Ann if she wants a shampoo! "Girlfriend," he says all soft and vomity, "Come on let Keithy do you. Make you some soap suds and run you some water." All the time he is rubbing his own chest the way men do when they are looking at women. I've seen it.

Soap bubbles and water running hypnotize Lee Ann, just the words alone, the words by themselves, so I was worried when Keith Peller starts talking trash about his shampoo and bubbles. He should practice his sex appeal and show off his chest with all its black curls, which do not go with his blonde hair except with the roots, to women his own age, which is twenty-nine, and leave girls alone, especially ones like Lee Ann, who is fifteen in years but only about half that in social skills and emotions or, to be mean, in the brains department.

Lee Ann has what Mama calls "her own ways," meaning epilepsy. She can understand many things, but we never know what she will take in or at what level. I know that it is sex and all "its ramifications" that has Mama the most worried about Lee Ann. Rape. Pregnant. As the kids say at school, these words are "key."

I wish Keith Peller would just try something weird with me, just try coming on to me! I would clean his clock with a few well-placed karate kicks that I have learned in gym class, plus I have my HIV move all planned, plus I will yell I'm having my period. But he won't try anything against a worthy opponent. At least, I think he has that much sense. Basically, he's a coward, but also evil and, therefore, very dangerous. He would never ask a normal girl, me for instance, if I wanted a shampoo. He chooses his victims, and that's the only sign of intelligence I see in him.

12

It'd be like asking if I'd like a tour of... what? I can't think of anything ridiculous enough. Maybe like asking a bear if he would like to be skinned. Alive. Or a river if it would like to dry up, or house if it'd like to burn, a beauty queen if she'd like psoriasis.

Seriously, no one should use what he knows about people who are sick the way my sister is to get a kiss, or worse, and maybe even get her in his van by turning her against her parents even if they are fosters.

If there were any true facts like alcohol or abuse to use against us and the way we take care of Lee Ann, then I would agree that Lee Ann should be taken away, but by a Ms. Karney and not by a Keith Peller in a van with Montana mountains painted on one side and Hawaiian surf on the other. There are places that are good, maybe as good as this home for Lee Ann. I doubt it, but maybe.

Walter—he's not my real father as I said—didn't even know Keith Peller was in the house, much less upstairs, and much, much less what he had in mind. I didn't know it either until he was there, smiling and saying, "Shhh....I won't hurt you if I don't have to. I don't want to hurt any girls. That's not what I have in mind."

Keith Peller can slip into places like a black snake and just be there along a ledge or under something. It is strange that man fears anything at all. He says it's snakes. I've heard him say that he can't even look at them in magazines. That he could face a gun easier than a snake. He may have to, I am thinking.

Who cares about his snake problem, I say, but I guess it's good to know that he is afraid of something on earth. I am surprised that it's snakes that're his problem, he's so much like one.

As old as he is, he still plays those war games where you pay to get shot with bags of paint. He comes away clean because of the way he can sneak-snake his way up on people.

That's exactly what he did two weeks ago. In the house, sneak-snake up the stairs, sliding into our room. I look up and there he is smiling as if he belonged there, saying "Shhh...I don't want to hurt any girls. No, no, that's not what I have in mind to do."

With me in charge while Walter was sleeping off the middle of a binge, which means that he was sleeping like a steel bar, while Mama's at work, I guess Walter was confident deep down under all of his sleep that I could keep things going along—people out of the house for instance—but just try keeping out a man who for over a year had the run of the place, though not of course since Uncle David's accident, if it was one, last summer.

"What that Keith Peller doesn't do, I would like to know," Mama has asked crying over the dish pan, and she didn't mean that he is a hair dresser, if he is one.

It was much easier when we had to worry just about Ms. Karney from the county office with papers with "Investigation and Family Structure Assessment" at the top. She even showed me the papers she needed on us, blank, before she filled them in. We have been added to her case load, and she is mad she has to drive all the way out here from the court house. She doesn't understand the first thing about us, but she has the power to ruin us, Mama says, and take away the

14

possibility of having Uncle David's boys come live with us. Of course, they haven't lived with us since the funeral. Ms. Karney will report to her supervisor who will "go before" the judge about whether we can provide a nurturing environment for Uncle David's three boys, the very environment they have always known and lived in.

Ernest is eight going on forty, Davey Jr. is four going on twenty, and James Howard is three and a wreck already, Mama says, if she doesn't get him back soon. She will cry over James Howard anytime, anywhere.

Ms. Karney doesn't know that Walter hates anyone connected to the government even when there is money for us involved. He wouldn't take it for himself, he says, and I know it's true.

I'm writing this story down. If I don't, I may forget a little detail that will make all the difference. At least to Mama and Walter when I'm dead and gone, though of course, they should be dead and gone before me.

I love writing those two words. Dead. Gone. They are so sad and very meaningful, and the things I write about will be more believable once they take shape in words, a million times more believable when they have been written by a dead person.

June 16

...I just read that paragraph from yesterday, and I love it even though "written by a dead person" sounds like I am dead or think dead people can sit up in their graves, in their nice metal coffins and write the truth about what happened while they were alive so that their families can come and pick up the typed pages rolling out at the stone markers on the graves and say things like "Now we understand. So that's what happened."

I wish dead people could write their stories, but they can't, so I will do the next best thing: write for them or about them. This book is dedicated to my Uncle David, but not to his boys because they are, excuse me for saying so, cousins from hell, even if I do want them to come back here to live. Part of me does. Part of me does not.

Uncle David's coffin looked like a file cabinet on its side. Of course, in real life, he had never been near a file cabinet that I can think of. He kept all his papers from his divorce and taxes in an old trunk he got at a yard sale. He refinished it so that its pine was a golden brown, a perfect toast color from a hundred years or more of just sitting in some godforsaken attic. And, of course, he couldn't type. I am sure he never wrote a letter in his life; he was a phone man. Loved to talk on the phone. Thought it was the world's greatest invention of all times, much better than the car, and we know what he thought of his cars! Lined up, shined down to their very souls, he would say, waxed to the point of moonlight.

I want to write about Uncle David's wedding before I write about his funeral, but writing is funny, and the wedding may have to wait because a funeral pushes ahead of a wedding in a writer's mind. Mama says that weddings and funerals have a lot in common. Uncle David's did. Mournful relatives for the groom, one friend for the bride, ditto for the funeral.

Broken-up relatives and friends for the dead man, one friend for the widow. That one friend would be, guess who, Keith Peller.

"Don't you have anyone else you would like to invite?" Mama asked Jeannine about the wedding.

Mama is polite at times when there is nothing else left to be.

"Not that I can think of," Ms. Jeannine Turner replied. She didn't count her daughter, Linda Jo, and who could blame her. She does not seem to be a member of the human family, was my thought at the time. None of those three seemed human, actually.

"However," as I love to write in my essays at school, they were acting miles more human at the wedding than they were just a little bit later, and of course, Uncle David was there making everyone happy at his own wedding. He had set up a kind of altar which was really a huge rock, already in place, as if it was meant to be an altar for a wedding, more of a small boulder on the bluff over the river, near the place where we had one year later what I call the last

17

picnic. There is an old, crooked sycamore tree there; its trunk has sheets of bark like paper peeling off.

Uncle David loved sycamores. He said Zacharias climbed one in the Bible to get a good look at Jesus over the crowd. "That's it," he said. "That's all I know about the Bible. But what I know I like. A man climbs a sycamore to see Jesus. When you think about it, there is a lot of wisdom to it—hidden in the story. Choice of tree for a good way to beat the heat and see the show—that tells you as much as anything in that story."

The day of the wedding I saw Keith Peller look at Jeannine when Uncle David was going on about the sycamore. At the time we were so busy—we had Uncle David's boys to deal with, and they are equal to at least thirty regular boys, and Mama was finishing the lattice work icing for the cake.

"How I regret that cake," she still cries. It was beautiful, much more than the one she made for Uncle David's first wedding to Mary Louise, an event I will write about if I run out of things to say about the second one, which I doubt seriously. I will just mention that at Uncle David's first, there was a crowd of people, close to a hundred, there was a roast pig stretched out on a rented silver tray on the table, and it was inside his new house, so the smells were wonderful—new house, roast pig, the hard breath of chrysanthemums from the huge iron pots of them along the rock walk to the house. Mama's cake was spread out, I mean the separate layers were put up on stands of various heights on a table with deep red roses arranged all through and around the glass columns holding the four cakes.

18

Mary Louise looked good. For her.

Of course, she had Ernest, the child she brought (from somewhere near Moscow or maybe hell, Walter said) to the marriage, and Ernest had worn her down—he was three just before the wedding—as he would wear us all down from that day on, but Mary Louise should have been counting her blessings.

She had not had, of course, her two new children, Davey Jr. and James Howard, with Uncle David.

I hope David is not the type of man who marries women who already have children, or women who expect me to throw them their wedding, Mama had said when he married Mary Louise, indicating that she did not think that this would be his only wedding. I repeated that to Uncle David when he laid it on us that he was going to marry Jeannine Turner.

He laughed and said he liked a good deal, a bargain, two for the price of one. One bride and one child he did not have the trouble of going to the hospital for. That was like Uncle David: to make the best out of the worst.

Linda Jo Turner, however, at her best, could never be seen as a bargain. Ernest was not, of course, a bargain either. His one talent was to throw up instantly. He could stop anything that was not going his way by pausing a second, looking down, and then, a fountain of orange and green would spurt up and out all over. He never got a drop of the vomit on himself. He back-stepped and curved his back into a bow so he was free and clear of the jet stream.

A child is never a bargain. I would never marry a man with a child. My husband and I will adopt our first

19

and maybe our only child to show what we think of adoption.

Back to Linda Jo Turner. Here is a story she told me, one that will mark her forever as the nutcase she is.

At her mother's wedding, a time when she should have chosen her words carefully, she walks up to me and starts right in the middle of a story about her mom's cousin, Brian Somebody, who got shot. Good, I wanted to say, one less of your family on earth, but I didn't. I wanted to hear how or why.

Now that I have a dead uncle, I feel something for all dead relatives, even Linda Jo Turner's, but at the time I could not have cared less about this dead cousin of theirs. It seems that this Brian was talking to his best friend who shot him twice, once in the wrist and once in the heart. I asked Linda Jo why the friend chose the wrist. The heart was the obvious target. Everyone thinks, she said, that the friend thought that Brian had stolen his watch. Didn't he ask Brian before he killed him, I couldn't help asking. She didn't know. A new watch was found in Brian's car.

I did not point out that she was kin to a thief because she seemed to think that Brian was innocent. I know now that dead people do seem more innocent than living ones. More innocent, more wise, more everything. A dying person is the best person to give you advice in my opinion. I would listen to every word a dying person was saying and write it down.

Uncle David was the best house painter in the state. They said he didn't even need to use drop cloths and could paint windows so clean they never needed to be scraped when he finished. He never taped the panes with masking tape either. He just turned his head to the side and got real close to the window. He dipped his brush a quarter of an inch into the paint bucket, and holding his hand steady, he used to say he "came on up the line," never touching the glass with even one hair of the paint brush. No one ever had to ask him to return and do touch ups. In the strongest light, no streaks, no skipped places, no drops from a heavy brush.

So, would a man like that, like my Uncle David, be so careless with his life that he would drown? I don't think so. As the kids at school say, "NOT."

Who is this "they," Mama cries, "who knows how David painted a window?" She is so pleased to hear about his good reputation as a painter even with her tears running like crazy, even with him dead and never able to paint again.

A metal coffin is five hundred dollars cheaper than the wooden one which Mama wanted. David loved wood, she kept saying. Well, he can't pay for it now, can he, I heard someone say, I forget who. The metal ones are watertight, though, and that convinced Mama to go with the metal.

I used to take Lee Ann to watch Uncle David paint. We'd sit in the middle of a big empty room and get him good stations on the radio. Country 102 or Q-94 he liked, but low enough for us to carry on a conversation. Sometimes he would ask us to get him the opera station for a change and a laugh, which we were glad to do.

21

I will try to tell the truth about how Uncle David just lay down deliberately on the bottom of the Willis River waiting to drown, while his kids, my cousins by adoption, and Mama and Walter and Lee Ann and I had ourselves a cookout (Jeannine and Keith Peller were there of course, in the vicinity, lurking), waiting for him to come back up the hill with a string of fish—bream to cook on a stick for those who like their fish burned black, or in a pan the regular way for the rest of us who like the fried crusts of the tail and fins. He had promised us all he'd bring back the fish and cook them the way we liked best.

Many times he has come back from the river swinging a line of wet fish dripping silver strips of water down his leg in the dirt leaving a trail.

Would a man who loved people waiting for him to bring them presents lie down and die in the middle of the afternoon, dead center in the middle of a picnic he helped plan, in a river so shallow it's really nothing but a creek?

I know there is a hidden and true story in what happened to us last summer. Uncle David must have been thinking something terrible, bad enough to make him lie down on the bottom of the river and die instead of doing all the things he had promised in one way or another—coming back with the string of fish (a small promise) and raising his kids (a big promise).

Some people explained the drowning by saying the drug people from the trailer court had hit him with a tire iron because of what he said to them about all of them swimming in his river off his sandy point, where the river forks and where this zip code on the map gets its name—Sandys Point, only it's named after a family, the high and mighty Sandys, not the river sand. But where were any tire iron marks on Uncle David's head?

People acted like they knew exactly what had happened, and the facts—no broken bones or bruises—didn't stop them from telling the story of the swinging tire iron and drug people. But the truth is that no one except Keith Peller was down at the river at the time except Uncle David, so all that those people really know is what did not happen and never would happen except in their heads but that makes it easier for them to think they understand how and why he drowned.

If people, drug dealers and users, black and white, couldn't lie to themselves as a hobby, they'd go crazy I guess.

Yes, I admit that I can see Uncle David saying something out of line to drug dealing people. That's entirely possible. He loved to talk out of line to everyone. Then, if the trailer court people had really been there at the river, I can see them saying something back, and I can even see the tire iron raised high or flying at his head if he had gone on too long.

But it's funny, this tire iron that left invisible marks and made no noise when it hit Uncle David and killed him, the only tire iron like it on earth.

I have seen Uncle David fishing with those trailer court people, and the only tire iron I saw was one they were using to help him pry off the flat tire from the rim when his truck picked up a nail. I have seen him borrow a chainsaw from Robert Pervall for a tree that had been struck by lightning and had fallen across the road, and many times I have seen them fishing together. Laughing, drinking beer. He painted the Pervall house. Didn't charge a dime.

Some say my uncle was too drunk to know he wasn't walking on land, that he thought the river was the path up the hill to the charcoal grill where we all waited on spread-out blankets held down by coolers and lawn chairs. Some said he was on the river bottom resting from his Jeannine, his new wife—it was five weeks to the day since the wedding—who had worn him out. They didn't mean just with sex, though that was part of what they meant, but with hard work. He was working himself to death for her. Maybe drowning himself, all of a sudden, was just a shortcut to the death that was coming if he kept up the way he was going.

I don't like to think of that wedding, but I will because I want to tell the truth. Uncle David cried at his second wedding. Of course, we did too, but that was natural because we could see what the bride was. Bad news. He was crying because he was so happy. Mama said she didn't blame him for crying if he had been crying for the right reason. The whole earth should have been crying, and it was. The rain was pouring down, straight from the sky, not slanted or slow. Ernest was running around like a wild man, setting off fire crackers and waving sparklers in the middle of the rain. He couldn't wait for night, and he got away with it because it was the wedding day, and Jeannine was not going to show her true colors to anyone, especially not to Uncle David's boys. She had Davey Jr. and James Howard eating out of her hand, had her picture made with her arms around them, Ernest standing tall and with his arm around her waist, James Howard sitting on her hip staring into the camera, not smiling, but trying to look his best. Davey Jr, looking up at her, drunk at the thought of a new mama in his life.

Maybe some idea just hit Uncle David like the tire iron that did not. Maybe he just lay down in the river to think about dying and died. I know I have been knocked off my feet by ideas, literally tackled from the back, sidelined, blindsided, so I know it can and does happen. I think that doctors do not know how to test for death brought on by a thought. Autopsies would not help.

Jeannine is pretty in an afternoon talk-show way. Everyone says so, everyone but Mama and me, but she's mean as a snake, as a nest of snakes. I know her, I believe, and will give one example of how she operated last summer, the snake part of her.

To my eye, she's not all that pretty, even as a bride, she had a glittery brightness to her that said something. It was more than the wet look she is so good at getting on her hair and lips. Now I know that Keith Peller was advising her on beauty, if he really does work in a hair place.

At the picnic, Jeannine took the last Coke from the old washtub filled with ice. She took it for herself when Sis, that's what I call Lee Ann sometimes, had not had the first taste, and was white around her lips and nose from helping me lug the big cooler full of the chicken up the hill. Mama sent the chicken to the cookout in case Uncle David didn't get the string of spot and bream he said he would pull out the river for us in three minutes.

Those were his words, the last ones to her. "Three minutes." Then he disappeared down the bluff that hangs over the river, and that was that.

Jeannine said she needed a Coke worse than any two kids did because she had forgotten her cigarettes, and she could bet, she said, that no one would run get her any. That was just about forty-five minutes before we knew Uncle David would be drowning that day.

It takes three minutes if water goes in the lungs, and not many people have the willpower to stay down in such shallow water. People talked about it as if, Mama said, there was something to be proud of in that kind of willpower. Before he got himself situated between the two big rocks, snagging his shoulders down, maybe while he was still looking for a good place to drown himself, Jeannine was being her usual hateful, selfish self.

We all thought he was getting us a string of fish. I guess as he was wading out to the rocks looking for a good place, a deeper place between rocks, she was taking that last Coke and opening it. Slow and in front of us, licking the brown foam up the frosty red can. We could drink the iced tea, she said, in the Igloo thermos, but she needed that Coke. This says it all about Jeannine in my opinion.

Ms. Karney heard about the "unfortunate incident" she called the drowning and started checking on us more than ever. She wanted to investigate how we were doing under the circumstances so she could write a report about whether Mama and Walter should be allowed to take (officially) Uncle David's three kids to raise. Ms. Karney had opinions about three more children added to our family dynamic, she called it. She had to clear us with her supervisor before the boys could come. She did not seem to listen to the fact that Mama had been raising those three boys all along from the day Mary Louise left them high and dry (and long before she left) until the day Uncle David drowned.

I doubt if Ms. Karney knows that Ernest is Mary Louise's son, but not Uncle David's, so we shouldn't have him anyway, but who else would want him or take him, Mama asks me.

Jeannine certainly never did anything that could be called even helping with the boys. Mary Louise, their own mother by blood, was not much better—she would cry a lot, so at least she was trying, we felt, but the work was always right there waiting for Mama and, I must say, me.

Even if your children are your own blood, even if you love them, there is more washing and cooking to be done than most Americans would believe.

At the funeral, Jeannine said she was taking her daughter Linda Jo, a blood daughter, and you can tell just looking at her, back to Roanoke Rapids. We could have David's boys. She even suggested that we send Ernest back to where ever Mary Louise's people were, since we were not obligated to him that she could see in any way. She said this the same way she said Lee Ann and I could have some iced tea while she drank the only Coke. She meant she didn't care who got those boys as long as she didn't, Mama said.

Mama sees Ernest as blood, though he is not really, but he has Uncle David's eyes, as we say around here, and he thought the sun rose and set in Uncle David, another local saying. In fact, Mama said it must have been Ernest that persuaded Uncle David to marry Mary Louise because no one in his right mind would have married her just for the pure fact of her herself. Of course, at the time we did not know Jeannine Turner, who makes Mary Louise look like a saint, a queen, a Mrs. Onassis, was waiting in the future to ruin our lives.

I guess it is a compliment that Mama thinks Lee Ann and I are as good as blood daughters. Uncle David's two sons by blood and Ernest, who was like his own son as I have said, have not budged Mama on the subject of blood, bad as those boys are, so maybe blood is not a big compliment. But her point was that the boys must come live with us legally or at least continue to live with us without the paperwork or until it went through, and the fact that Jeannine did not want the boys was of no importance.

Mama loves to add that phrase, "of no importance." The fact that we wanted the boys to stay on with us would be too simple, Walter said, for the government mind, for Ms. Karney. We'd have to prove that we have a suitable home for them. It suited the boys for years just fine, Mama says, but facts don't matter to the government, Walter says, or to many people.

We have to prove that we have a good home now. We have to prove that the front porch is not rotting off and that the pipes do not freeze in the winter, that we have central heat and central air instead of areas of heated and cooled space in the house. Walter says he can't do everything by himself. He means that Uncle David would have known how to jack up the foundation of this old house and put in insulation, how to put temporary columns up on the porch and then permanent ones, how to install electric heat ducts. Ms. Karney lives in a condo townhouse and she looks at this house as if it were some inner city project where anything terrible can happen. She may have that right.

I wish we did live in a city, even an inner city sometimes.

And I wouldn't mind if some other children did come to live with us. Some nice ones. Maybe they could help out with Lee Ann some. Maybe Uncle David's boys inherited their daddy's interesting personality and sweet ways about him and those traits have not come out yet. Ernest was beginning to pick up on some of those traits and to copy the way Uncle David walked, tilted forward as if something great were going on just over the next hill.

Lee Ann will look better when the swelling around her lips goes down and the bruises fade. For that matter, so will I.

Here's what happened, really happened when Keith Peller returned in the flesh, roaming in our house, trying to get to Lee Ann, not thinking that I would be there.

It went like this: Lee Ann falls down the steps and wakes Walter up. He does not like to wake up all at once from noise, especially if he's in the middle of a binge. His room is backed up against the steps. So suddenly, there is a loud noise right at his head. Maybe it even shakes his head a little through the wall.

Lee Ann won't cry, which is one of the weird things about her. At Uncle David's funeral she just kept patting the casket, walked right up to it while we were singing his favorite hymn, "Just As I Am," but never made a sound. Mama's sister, Helen, who had driven thirty-one hours from Houston, made up for that. She cried so hard she fainted, and I had to help her walk out of the church and over to the grave. She wrote us a letter and said she would never forget how sweet I was that day when I was having trouble breathing and walking and living myself and was worried that Mama wouldn't make it even with Walter half carrying her.

Yes, I will say that Aunt Helen fell for Lee Ann and me all over again at the funeral and made us swear to run away to live with her. We were our own baby-selves, she kept saying, meaning that we had not lost our sweet baby souls by growing up. Of course, she was wrong, but it was nice to hear and nicer of her to see us that way. She did not know how much her invitation to come live with her meant to me or really what she was saying in her brokenhearted rattling on because that is what I am thinking I must do to get Lee Ann away from Keith Peller: Go to Texas.

Aunt Helen always has a joke, and even at the funeral of her baby brother—she called him The Baby—when she hyperventilated from crying, she was saying things that some people could not understand. Before the funeral when people were walking up to view him (it is called "view"), Aunt Helen bent over Uncle David and said down to his face, "Good as you look, Baby, you won't be marrying a third time, I guess. Those girls' eyelashes are wasted on you now."

We all know how to take Aunt Helen's jokes, but some people don't and get mad or can't see the humor. She might have a gene missing, Angela says, who has read up on gene therapy and serial killers who might also. Aunt Helen might not have a clue about how she comes off to people. To me, she is funnier than anything, and I know Uncle David would have loved what she said to him in the casket. Jeannine did not think it was a bit funny, but she'd break her face if she smiled or even looked like she might. I have seen her practice her look, the over-the-shoulder one, in the mirror for as long as eighteen minutes. I could not stand to look at my face if it was hers that long.

The only noise Lee Ann made when she was falling down the steps was her body hitting the wood. Most people would cry or scream or groan. Me, I didn't scream or anything either as I watched her go down, shoulders and head bumping hard, her face taking the worst of it, because I knew I was already in enough trouble.

I was dumb enough to hope that Walter would not wake up, somehow. I was thinking if I only could get Keith Peller out the house and into his hideous van that he thinks is so cool, then I could clean up Lee Ann and we could go on with the day as if nothing terrible had happened.

The truth is this, and I can say it in this book: The situation was bad, in the old sense. I had a drunk who was waking up (Walter) and a drinking man (Keith Peller) upstairs in the bedroom with my epileptic sister. "Furthermore," as I love to write almost as much as "however" in my essays at school, Lee Ann did not have on many clothes and Keith Peller, as I said, was drinking and as usual had rape stashed somewhere in the frontal lobe of his brain.

Seeing Lee Ann's broken teeth and blood shocked and sobered Walter up instantly. Keith Peller vanished. He did. Out the back window, down the back porch roof like a spider or his favorite animal, a snake. Same way he had come in.

When Walter calmed down—that night—and after he had worked me over good, he talked about how he was going to put in a whole new staircase, one not as steep as a ladder propped against a floor joist like the g.d. one we had. He must have been thinking automatically, even after a year, that David would help him build the new staircase. They had a hundred plans for restoring this house, but first they had built Uncle David's house, then there were delays for him and Mary Louise to have those two babies—Davey Jr. and James Howard. That took a lot of time, and then Mary Louise got worse, cried all the time instead of part of the time, and walked off, deserted them. That took up some more time. Then Keith Peller and Jeannine Turner showed up, and the rest is history.

So this house looks exactly like it did the day some Confederate soldiers got lost looking for Appomattox, except for some primitive wiring and plumbing. The soldiers slept in the yard, and it must be true because we have found some stuff they were using for bullets.

By the time Walter got out the bed and into the front hall, no one could have made him believe that I had not let Lee Ann fall down the stairs. My hand looked nailed to the banister and felt that way too. Me at the top, Lee Ann crumpled up at the bottom.

In fact, Walter got it in his head that I had picked some kind of fight with Lee Ann and had knocked her out, though when has that ever happened? His head was not working right because of being mid-binge, and I'm not saying I haven't wanted to knock her flat, deck her with one slap, do a Bruce Lee number on her, but wanting and doing are very different. It looked as if Lee Ann had been pushed down the splintery stairs, and that a fight between a poor, afflicted, handicapped foster child and another vicious, healthy foster child who did not appreciate all that had been done for her by her foster family was what woke him up. I knew I could not argue with Walter in his condition. A bear disturbed in the middle of deep hibernation. A drunk grizzly.

So, what we had was Walter still too close to a mile-deep sleep when he saw Lee Ann in a sprawl and me standing at the top of the stairs looking dead-to-rights like the one who had shoved her own sister from the top step and maybe killed her. I had just jerked my arms back and grabbed the newel post with my left hand. The sight of me safe at the top got him going, and Lee Ann in a heap, bleeding in silence at the bottom ignited the gasoline in his heart.

I did not mention Keith Peller. I felt terrible because in a way I was protecting him, but I had to protect myself, and the only way to do that was to cover for him.

Walter did hold off from slapping me until he got Lee Ann cleaned up, so he was not as hot as he could have been. But then he let go.

No, she had been pushed. It's true, she had not fallen. These are the facts. I did push my sister down the steps, but I did not mean for her to knock her teeth out. That part was an accident. I was saving her from Keith Peller.

Lee Ann likes to compare blue and yellow bruised skin the way girls compare tans at school. I have some pretty good ones on my arms now where Walter grabbed me. All he ended up doing was rattling my bones, two or three big shakes and a few yanks on my arms. It looks worse than it was, and Ms. Karney would go ballistic if she saw me. Lee Ann's falls are what she expects though she looks suspicious sometimes. I am not supposed to look abused, and most of the time I don't. I was yelling about tripping and an accident so loud that, to shut me up, Walter quit working on me.

Lee Ann is eligible for front teeth according to Ms. Karney, but we have to wait for the paperwork to go through, she says. While we are waiting, I don't have much else to do, and I found this old composition book that had just a few pages used up, so I'm starting my book, "Dead and Gone." It's the best title I have ever heard. It won't have a murder in it, because as I have said there were no marks on Uncle David to make the sheriff think he had been murdered, but there will be a dead person, an intruder, and, I hope, runaway girls.

Uncle David is lying on the bottom of the river—everything is wrong with that picture.

34

Keith Peller was with him. Some friend he turned out to be. We tried to tell Uncle David that he was dealing with a first class loser, but men are funny about their friends. I guess because they are so rare, so hard to find, so when they find one, they think they have found a precious stone. I have heard Mama tell the story a hundred times since last summer when it happened, and of course, I was there on the bluff waiting for those "three minutes" and the fish to grill or pan fry. Being present does not always help with understanding things, and understanding things will not fix them or change them.

Uncle David was so drunk, people said, that they bet he just sat on those rocks laughing at something we didn't know about and still don't. He was so good at drinking, no one could tell when he was drunk except Mama and me. She remembers Keith Peller yelling, "David is so drunk, he's just resting in the river using rocks for pillows." I can't believe anyone would yell that—it sounds too poetic. Drunks are often poets, I know from English class, but Mama says she heard "rocks for pillows" every word of it. Keith Peller was drunk himself, as usual, so maybe he did know. Takes one, Mama and I say, to know one.

Uncle David had trouble not only in choosing his friends, but his wives. Bad and worse were his two choices, Mama says, so he did not have much chance for a good life in this world, and it is a miracle he lived as long as he did. Thirty-four years.

I have a drowned uncle buried here in Virginia, my Aunt Helen and an unknown daddy down in Texas, and a mother—a blood one—who left me twelve years ago for Salt Lake City to become a Mormon so she could sing in the famous choir. She had a pretty voice, a very pretty one, and face too. She just couldn't go out there with a baby. Me.

I look like her, Mama and Aunt Helen say, but I better not, they say, act like her, running off leaving a baby. Mama knew my real mother from living in a trailer next to her duplex, and that's how she came to know me. Aunt Helen was down the street then; in fact, she knew my mother first and introduced her to Mama before I was born, when my mother knew I was on the way. And when Aunt Helen met me, she says I looked into her eyes as if I understood her better than anyone she had ever known, so it was at that moment she knew that I belonged to her in a way, at least to her family. We are kindred spirits. She could not take me even though she wanted to worse than anything on earth because Ellis—she had just married him after years of his begging her to—had lost his job, and they did not know if they could keep body and soul together, but June, her sister, needed a new baby to help her broken heart over Lee Ann's condition. That would be me.

I helped everybody and everything, Aunt Helen swears, and Mama does too when she is not suffering so from all that has happened and can remember how lucky she was to get me. Aunt Helen knows me and said at Uncle David's funeral for me not to forget where I had a second home, as did Lee Ann. She wishes we would all come back to Texas, and I told her, both of us crying like crazy, that I did too.

No, I did not come through any agency like regular adopted babies. I was a friend, more than one. Lee Ann was too, but she did not come from as close a friend as I did. Aunt Helen sized up Keith Peller and Jeannine in one second. She told Mama and Walter that she knew that they could not be held responsible for the world's trash, but she was shocked to find it in our family. She said this sympathetically so Mama did not lose her temper, and she was too brokenhearted anyway at the funeral and just shook her head and said "How true, Helen." Ellis did not make the trip for the funeral because he had just started a new job and this was the one that would take them to Australia. He has his dreams, Aunt Helen laughs, and says the nice thing about him, one of them, is that he wants to take us all with him. He was very close in his way to Uncle David. Admired him. Who wouldn't?

June 17

...When this book called DEAD AND GONE is found, everybody at the sheriff's office or funeral home will say to Mama and Walter, "That daughter of yours, Crystal, saved your other daughter's life. Didn't Lee Ann run off the day of the accident at the river? Didn't your Crystal find her? You could have ended up on television begging for information."

It's a joke at school about television and lost-runaway kids. Any lost-kid joke they love. I don't know if grown-ups like jokes about lost kids. Probably not, even though they should, when you think about it, because it's grown-ups who steal kids. It's not kids stealing kids. I guess people don't like to joke about what they do bad. For instance, do you ever hear a kid joking about failing a grade? Maybe once in a blue moon, and usually it's after he has grown up and made a couple of million in construction or franchises. Oh, right. Then he looks back and laughs at failing the fourth grade, feeling free.

There's so much to think about and try to explain. How neither Lee Ann or I am a real daughter, not a blood daughter. Why Mama and Walter wanted to adopt another baby that would be me, after they saw the first signs of what could go wrong with a baby (Lee Ann) you don't know much about. Lee Ann slept too long. We know that now, but at the time, Mama says, she just took it as a good sign and a blessing on them all.

I do not know all the details about how I came into Mama and Walter's life, but I do know that they got me as part of a friendship with my real mother who wanted to sing in Utah, which I have said. I guess I was pretty, even as a brand new baby, so they couldn't resist me. Or maybe it was the sad story of how my real daddy had gone off just before I was born, leaving my real mother with her nice voice and face and wanting to sing in the Tabernacle Choir. She writes to me once a month, or tries to, if her schedule permits. Her letters could be used for movie documentaries, they are so detailed. She is someone who enjoys trips and can find interesting things to report on. She says a person can sink in Salt Lake, contrary to what we have heard. She has tried and did. It's a nine-mile hike to the bottom of the Grand Canyon. College boys never grow up if they go work in Jackson Hole, Wyoming. She knows a lot of very interesting things about life in America because of her travels. I keep her letters under the lamp by my bed so I can reread them. She does not know about Lee Ann's condition and thinks I am living a very "nurtured" life with her friends June and Walter. And I am in a way. One of my teachers loves the word "interesting" which she pronounces in a way I love, "inTRESting," sounding Britishy or ETV-y, and that is the word I think describes my life. Mama says we should not tell my mom about Lee Ann because it would worry her and she is a fragile person. It helps me to know I am helping my real mother.

39

Angela warns me not to let that feeling carry me away. Helping parents can be dangerous, even fatal mentally or physically, she says, and adds, as if I did not know every detail about her life, that she is an expert, being the only child to people who need all the help they can get. She does not mind helping her parents, and I help them too when I can, but when Angela is through with college where she will go on full financial aid plus scholarships, like me, which we have planned, she says she is out of there, out of their lives except for an occasional visit when they are sick.

It was nice when Ms. Karney first started coming around after Uncle David drowned, when she was just checking us out in a general way about whether his boys could live here and before she saw what she was looking at with us, "in all our glory," Mama says, meaning with all our problems. It was nice to have Ms. Karney trying to get close to Lee Ann and me, her putting cotton between our toes getting ready to paint them Lady Slipper Pink by Avon. It helped pass the time. Of course, all the time it was written all over her what she was doing: trying to decide if Uncle David's boys could be "placed" here. Mama said for me "to guard against insinuation," meaning that some people will do anything to get close to you. Mama was at work, and Ms. Karney was making "yet another" of her "surprise visits" trying to catch us in our natural habitat, see an abusive relationship or "gauge," as she says for other things, how bad Walter's drinking was.

The truth is that Walter is one of those alcoholics who get nicer and nicer the more he drinks. No one believes it, but it's true. He mellows, Angela calls it.

40

Doesn't smile like a fool, like a Keith Peller, but only gets kinder or milder. Discusses points in history like whether Roosevelt started World War II. Explains things. Of course, he is fierce underneath all that smiling and discussing, and he cannot be disturbed from the sleep he crashes down into. But for the most part, he is a nicer man drunk than otherwise. I did not say a better man, just nicer. Cold sober, between binges, he "stares into the abyss" (his words) and "does not like what he sees." Mama understands him. She regrets the condition, but because her own father drank, she understands.

I know one thing. In Virginia, time is as slow as it must be at the South Pole, except it's hot here. Mama keeps the AC going, but we have just one unit and that's in Walter's room. He's sleeping most days and working nights, and like I said, I am the one in charge. Mama has picked up a week's work, debeaking chickens, so she's gone. I begged to go work with her. Other kids from school debeak and I know I could learn, and when Mama heard you got paid by the bird, she almost let me go, but who would watch Lee Ann?

So, entering the eighth grade this fall, and a member of the Gold Club, which means all A's, I am stuck in this falling down house with a bruised, epileptic sister with missing teeth.

Pushing Lee Ann down the steps really helped the situation. I'll stick by that till I'm dead. Or gone.

If Mama or Walter had seen what I saw, I don't know what would happen now. I guess they might have called the sheriff. Then, we never would get Uncle David's boys, a thought that in itself is a temptation, and we might lose Lee Ann because it would look like we do not protect her.

Lee Ann can learn to smile without showing her teeth or where they were. Anyway, she may get some new ones. I'll teach her to smile, mysterious like, without opening her lips at all. She's sleeping most of the time anyway on her new medicine.

How was I to know she'd fall on her teeth, on her face, down the steps? A normal person would have sense enough to tuck her head down when she fell. "Tuck it in," I wanted to yell, but couldn't because I would wake up Walter. If I had yelled at all, I should have yelled something like "Help!" or "Ms. Karney, stop pushing my sister down the steps!" I guess it would have been better for Walter to think Ms. Karney was upstairs than for him to know who really was upstairs. If he had known, if he knew now, that Keith Peller had his ugly self up there poking around Lee Ann, Keith Peller would be dead now, and Walter would be on death row waiting for the electric chair.

And how would I have produced Ms. Karney out of thin air after yelling her name? What good would it have done for me to yell out the truth: "Keith Peller is here, upstairs, trying to rape, or something like it and without going to much of the trouble that is usually connected with raping someone, Walter!"

I have found that truth is not all that helpful. I know people swear it is, and I love it in small personal doses. But I cannot see how telling this big true thing, and calling it what it is—attempted rape (in italics, please) or attempted, because I prevented it—would help anyone. Keith Peller is an expert at these

42

crimes—drowning last summer and then attempted rape this summer.

You'd think Lee Ann would know all there is to know about falling. Another thing she doesn't know is about letting people influence her against the people who love her.

She does not realize that Ms. Karney has big plans for her.

I heard Ms. Karney tell Mama that I was too young to have to look after Lee Ann so much. That's why Ms. Karney invited Lee Ann to go off with her in the car, to give me a break. Mama said, and she was right, that Crystal Annette Ball (my beautiful whole name that my real mother gave me in Texas—not many people know about my middle name. I know they laugh at Crystal Ball, but they think Crystal is pretty, which it is, but the whole name is very beautiful) didn't need any break. Crystal Annette Ball had plenty of break time. She was the one, Mama was getting mad, who could use a break.

June 18

...Then Ms. Karney asked Mama if she didn't want to talk about it, and that's when Mama went into how we had moved up here to Virginia from Texas where I'm going back to when I'm sixteen (before then if I can arrange everything) and can drive. I won't worry now about whose car I will be driving. Before Texas, they had lived in Ohio, before she got strapped with two adopted daughters.

I'll be glad to take Lee Ann with me to Texas where people are nice when they are sober. They laugh a lot and tell stories. They work mostly in the daytime. My blood relatives are there, Aunt Helen's in-laws who are as Texan as is possible, she says, and Lee Ann's too, different relatives from mine, but I know I can find them. Social workers aren't all like Ms. Karney. I know they have better rules in Texas.

Mama was afraid when she got home and heard about the accident that the nerves would be hanging out of the teeth, but Walter thought the medication Lee Ann was on would prevent any pain. Walter went on and on about how he was not going to have a kid, by which he meant me, rough housing and romping and that I could stay in my room for a while.

I could tell Mama was glad, because with me on restrictions, she can leave Lee Ann with me without feeling too guilty and go out to work. Debeaking chickens or staying with old ladies that nobody else will, ones that wear diapers like babies and can't eat by themselves—these are her best paying jobs. It's funny when you think about it that they trust me with Lee Ann, after I, or so they claim, broke her teeth. It's even funnier, not ha ha, that no one thought a thing in this world about the possibility that Keith Peller was anywhere near the house, much less upstairs. Walter really didn't see or hear him vanish, but I did. Vanishing is not necessarily silent, especially if you know what is happening. I heard him push through the screen in my window, the screen he had slit with his hunting knife when he came in, though I did not hear him because I was asleep. The screen is something I will have to explain. I guess Keith Peller got himself out and onto the back porch roof and then off into the woods.

In Texas, I think we would be happier. I think if I got Lee Ann and me all the way down there to Aunt Helen's that Mama and Walter would follow us, maybe not right away, but eventually. We could start new lives in Texas. Before all this trouble, Mama was taking Lee Ann and me to watch the old ladies with her. I was in charge of Lee Ann, letting her have a cigarette out in the car when she woke up enough from her pills, so she wouldn't burn herself or the car. Mama and I don't let her smoke in anybody's house, not ours either, just the car.

June 19

...This is not our house. We still have a duplex in Houston. Mama is trying to sell it long-distance, with the help of Aunt Helen, who still lives in half of it (LUCKY), but no one wants it, she says, because of the water problem. Mama gets letters she has to sign for all the time. She cries and yells at me and Lee Ann and the next thing we know, she has us going on one of her day jobs. There are a bunch of fees when you sell a house in Texas. In Virginia you couldn't give a house away, much less ask money for it. Maybe one of the big ones, half-brick and half-board with columns. Maybe you could unload one of those and charge people to come look at how dumb and lonely it looked sitting out in a field, with a river you can't see just beyond the trees, not a 7-Eleven or any kind of store in sight.

This house is not one with columns because they rotted down with the front porch. It is all wood over a hundred years old which looks like what it is, a wrecked wreck. If the back porch had rotted any more, Keith Peller might have broken his ankle when he jumped out the window.

I have told Angela about what happened; she is the only person. I had to write her a letter because I can't use the phone for the next twenty years. She wrote back and was smart enough to type my name and address on a label so it looked like junk mail and I got

46

it without Mama or Walter asking any questions. Not that they would care if I got a letter from Angela Marks, but they might think of the "principle" of being grounded, remember that they were mad at me, put the letter on the mantel piece and not let me read it until I was forty-five.

Angela said in her letter that I had witnessed an actual defenestration. I must write back somehow and correct the impression I gave her that I had actually seen Keith Peller slit the screen and squeeze himself through, out onto the roof of the porch like Zorro, and leap down silent as a thief which he is. I wish to Jesus I had seen it, but I did hear the zip of the knife cutting the screen wire, then the pushing through of those bony shoulders and big head of hair, and those long legs. I was busy pushing Lee Ann up off the bed and out into the hall and then down the stairs so I could not witness the defenestration. Angela won't mind and will remind me of an old Russian proverb about no one lies as well as an eye witness, and she will give me credit for hearing the defenestration. We are like bird watchers. We give ourselves credit for our unusual experiences, as extracurricular training for the lives we want to lead. I got extra points for being in the presence of an attempted rape, and Angela agrees that that is exactly what it was, and that, of course, is worth more than escaping through a window. I got two hundred points for preventing the rape.

There is nothing to recommend this house except that it is rent-free. Walter and Uncle David were going to fix it. I'm not supposed to tell anybody it's rent-free, but couldn't anybody tell just by looking at it: the porch rotten, the windows broken, the floor boards up and down? Walter's going to fix it, all right. By himself? I'll be a hundred and never have friends over. I can't talk about Lee Ann either, so if I ever had my friends come over, what would I say when Lee Ann hid behind the door and stuck her head out, now with no front teeth, and smiled? "That's my sister, but not my real one?" I can't talk about the drowning either, so that leaves me with this book, DEAD AND GONE, to talk to, to talk in. Not counting writing to Angela.

Mama says for me to quit explaining to everyone that I'm adopted because nobody cares where I came from. Just be glad I have a roof over my head and food to eat. Not a very good roof, I want to say. But now I will just write it down. Not a very good roof. They think they can fix up this old wreck without Uncle David, but I have serious doubts. Put in new steps that curve around the hall like the old ones used to before vandals came and removed them because Hessian soldiers had carved the banisters. The stairs were long gone when we arrived on the scene and Uncle David and Walter rigged up these steep, ladder-like ones. Walter wants the new stairs to slant some instead of going straight up. That's Walter's idea of what he's going to fix up first. Mama would like the old circular stairs back. "In another life," Walter says.

What he calls the cat fight Lee Ann and I had on the steps will force him to think about better stairs.

June 20

...I heard Mama say she'd give her arms, both of them, to know why her brother drowned himself. She knows it could not have been to get out of raising those three boys—that is what he wanted to do in the house he had built. He didn't mean to drown himself, I am sure, but that's what it adds up to, she says, that he deserted his own children. She is angry at him even though she cries all the time.

Mama is starting on Jeannine again. You'd think that a year would take her mind off Jeannine if not off the drowning. She gets going on the subject and can't stop. Any little thing can start her up. A good example is the word key, which reminds her of Keith Peller. Walter and I are careful never to say key. He used to lose his truck keys, but not anymore, or anyway he never uses the word "key." This old house has never been locked. Why lock up a pile of rotten wood? So I don't have much use for the word key myself. Keith Peller's been gone since the funeral, Mama says, not knowing that she is wrong about him. But Mama has a talent for thinking about things, and especially people, who are not here. That is why she has so many pen pals. Twenty-six. New Zealand, France, Turkey, Wales. Even somewhere in Africa, there is a black woman, but Mama says she's really British and whiter than anyone she knows. Then she says that lately in her life she's seen worse white ways than black ones, so it's no compliment to her pen pal in Durban. All the pen pals write in English, not very good English, but Mama says they can't help it because they are foreign born. We don't give Mama anything for presents but stamps, money for stamps, or that crinkly writing paper. She says all she wants is pen pal stuff.

June 21

...Mama says Jeannine divided up the boys into foster homes so fast after the funeral it made her sick to her stomach, even though she had said in so many words that we could have them, but then she probably thought that she would have a straighter shot at the house and the money she got from selling it if Uncle David's boys weren't living next door in a wreck of a house. With Ms. Karney talking about all the regulations about children, even nephews, Mama did not know what to do, how to stop Jeannine. "Heart of stone, eye of gravel, hands of glass," Mama kept saying the day Jeannine drove off with Uncle David's boys all lined up in the backseat of her car, bathed and dressed in the same clothes they wore to the funeral. She tricked them into thinking they were all going to King's Dominion. Ernest waved his solemn wave to us; Davey Jr. stared straight ahead, and James Howard copied Ernest by giving a floppy little wave. "Little do they know," Mama kept saying. She was right. Straight to the Children's Home for temporary, Jeannine called it, custody, while she made her plans (sell Uncle David's house, get the money, cut and run).

Mama should give me more credit for having Lee Ann on me. Who changes her sheets every morning and starts her getting dressed? Every little thing she forgets overnight, it looks like to me. I put her shoes right under her feet, and she cannot for the life of her remember she has to point her toes. She stomps her heels down on the shoes and tries to grind them on. It's never going to work, I tell her.

One time I split the toe of her tennis shoes, so she could put on her shoes the way she wanted, stomping down and then working her toes in. Who helped her "tame" a hummingbird and learn from that how to put on her shoes better sometimes? I knew when to watch at Mama's Rose of Sharon bush where a hummingbird comes. Lee Ann thought that when he stood still in the air it was because he was tame and wasn't afraid of us. Then she would hold her feet like little hummingbirds over her shoes.

Jeannine thought coming back for the dedication of the tombstone was really something and would make up for the way she had acted when the rescue squad had finally gotten to the river the day Uncle David "got out of raising those boys," as Mama says in her mean voice. Jeannine also might have thought coming to the dedication would help with the fact that she kicked the boys out of their own house, the one their dead (and gone) father had built by himself, not counting Walter's help. She sold it the week after the funeral, and now she and Linda Jo have sixty-eight thousand dollars in cash, and the boys got...guess how much...Not a penny. Don't get me started on Linda Jo Turner or you'll be sorry. Stuck on herself! She'd make a dog laugh, the way she walks. Now she is rich and I guess much worse than she was, if that is possible, not that I have seen her.

June 22

...I will write down the story of Uncle David's drowning once and then go on. I don't want to be like Mama in that way—not able to get past something. I don't want to keep on retelling things over and over. Walter has told her if she can't quit, he's going to leave and take Lee Ann and me with him. She says go ahead, and I yell he'll have to find me and Lee Ann first because, bad as this old falling down house is, it's better than living in a truck, which is where we would be living, eating little cans of things Walter likes with raw onions. I think he's just talking to hear himself. Men are like that.

Jeannine had been carrying on foolishness, flirting with Keith Peller who was so bad off (drunk) he couldn't keep his van on the road when they left the picnic. He and Jeannine had driven off a little while before we actually knew that Uncle David was on the bottom of the river.

Important things happen so unimportantly. First, Keith Peller had come back up the hill, grabbing hold of the paw paw trees to work his way up to us on the blankets. The Johnson grass was so flattened down by the night's rain and so slick and wet, we had us a nice sliding place from the blankets down to the riverbank. It would have been a great picnic day except for what happened.

Then Keith Peller said to Jeannine, who was drinking our last Coke when he got back up the hill, "Let's me and you go get some beer." He was smart enough, now that I think about it, to say at that point to Jeannine, "Linda Jo can go with us." He didn't mean it, and she did not go, but it was smart to seem interested in a young person—often a disguise for evil. He talked like he had river water inside his head, rolling around, but it was really whiskey and beer. He had slept on a blanket on the back porch with his bottle of Rebel Yell poking up between his legs. Mama said it was disgusting and made me and Lee Ann use the back door after he fell asleep long before dark so we wouldn't have to look at him. Mama couldn't understand why Walter put up with the likes of Keith Peller. "He's your brother's friend, that's why," he always said.

"But you got them together," she said. "David never heard of Keith Peller until he came here with you one night after work, and the same goes for Jeannine Turner too." She came here with that drunk Peller man and got David drinking, when he had been doing so good on his own without that sorry wife of his, Mary Louise. Then Walter yells, "June, you are right again. I invented the birds and bees. I made it happen. And speaking of those things, you better wake up and smell the coffee, and get Lee Ann an operation before there is a baby around there." The baby operation always makes Mama cry and shuts Walter up. He sobers up at the thought of somebody getting pregnant. The fight is over when the words "baby operation" kick in.

54

In Health and Community Class, I have learned all about sex and getting pregnant, and I know it is impossible to get pregnant if you are mature and responsible.

The day Uncle David drowned I was sitting with Lee Ann keeping her quiet and patient and from wandering off in the woods. I couldn't give her another pill until two on the dot, but I wanted to because she was getting so "thrashy." That's what we call the way she starts throwing her head and arms as far as she can away from her body. It's like she wants to throw her arms and head away. Sometimes her legs too. When Walter is in a good mood, he calls it break dancing, an old term from his era. My job was to stuff a clean towel in her mouth and to watch out so that she didn't show her underpants (if she had any on because lately she's been taking them off without me knowing). Close to pill time, she can get real bad, fast.

Mama was setting up the grill for the chicken, saying we could forget the fish if we had been counting on any. It was one of those high windy days up on the grassy bluff over the river. It all would have made a good movie if we had been better looking. Because I'm adopted, I look pretty good, but Mama has let herself go, which is the way Jeannine described all people other than herself. It's true about Mama. "Three minutes, my foot," Mama kept muttering.

The river was very low, even with the big rain the night before, a shiny, clear brown and the sycamores were dragging their big leaves in the water. We were sliding down the soft Johnson grass path on plastic trash bags and the blankets folded on top of the bags.

55

When we got to the river, I would swing down into the water from a tree branch. Lee Ann enjoyed watching everything and she loved the sliding until she started getting thrashy, so I brought her back up the hill to rest and wait for the chicken and fish, if Uncle David ever caught any, to be grilled.

Uncle David had his fishing boat tied to the trunk of one of the big trees. They had to use that rope to pull him up the hill. Mama wrapped him up in the cotton quilt and that's what Jeannine and Keith saw, a wrapped-up dead person, which they didn't know was one at first, when they got back from the store with the beer.

The Rescue Squad had a winch, but their rope wasn't long enough to go all the way down the bluff to the river. I think it is terrible that they had to use Uncle David's own rope to pull him in.

Just as we were beginning to get worried, I slipped Lee Ann her pill so I could leave her by herself and go down and look myself for Uncle David. She was crying because she thought I was sneaking in another grass slide down to the river. "See," I said, "I'm leaving both our sliding bags here on our blanket." She couldn't say anything then. She understands some things perfectly.

Nobody had to look for Uncle David long because he was wedged between two rocks in water about two feet deep, just enough for the empty boat. You had to go down river about a mile to use a boat most of the time because of the lines of falls. We could see his blue jeans under the water. Mama said nothing looks worse than drowning victims, and I agree.

The men got him dirty dragging him uphill even with the quilt wrapped around him. Walter crawled beside him and would lift his head up so it wouldn't hit on the rocks. He was crying.

And that's the story of Uncle David's drowning.

June 24

...When the tombstone was ready, Jeannine had
stopped by the foster homes and picked up Ernest,
Davey Jr. and James Howard to bring to the dedication
service at Mt. Zion. That's not our church. We don't
have one, but the Baptists let us use Mt. Zion, and a lot
of them came even though they didn't know us. The
ceremony of putting up the tombstone was held at an
odd time–2:30 on Tuesday, August 9. I guess that was
the time no one else much wanted the church. They
had let us have the funeral in June there, so they more
or less had to go on let us have the follow-up
dedication service, Mama figured. Uncle David
thought he left his body to science. He had it printed
on his driver's license, but Mama said that meant only
if he was killed on the highway, not if he were at
home, so to speak, when he went, and since he was at
home, she was going to see him in the ground the
right way and not have him cut up in a lab down at the
Medical College. We had to pay three hundred
twenty-five dollars for a plot in the Mt. Zion cemetery,
which is worth every penny because the graveyard is
beautiful and sits right in a hilly curve with the
headstones all facing the road. They keep the grass
cut, and every holiday there are lots of wreaths put
out. It is so pretty.

Jeannine acted exhausted from driving the three boys down to the service. She thought the tombstone with David's picture slipped into the front of the built-in vase was going to impress everyone, but it didn't. No one could believe that a photograph even in plastic melted around it could last a year. No more than a month, Mama thought.

I don't want Uncle David's boys to come back here, but I don't want Ms. Karney to say we are not fit to have them. It was bad enough when they were here before with Mary Louise. Maybe I should be more sympathetic to Mary Louise, pregnant or depressed all of her four years of married life to Uncle David, and then you throw in living half the time with us in this wreck of a house and half the time in the new house while Uncle David worked on it. "His house" she used to say. "It's the House of David." You felt her bitterness hit you like squirts of lime or lemon juice when you pinch the rind and zing someone in the eye. I never understood what was so terrible about having someone build you a house, but she said I was too young.

But back to the problems of now. Ernest and Davey Jr. and even James Howard are older and would tease Lee Ann to death, not that she'd care. She stopped talking so long ago I am the only person who can remember how she sounds.

On the other hand, maybe a bunch of boys, wild and mean as they are and older now by a year, would lift Mama's spirits and would keep Walter from going on so many binges. When the boys came back here after the tombstone dedication, they crawled up the trees and onto the roof so they could peek in at people changing out of their church clothes. No one knew, but me, how they got up on the roof. "Jumped from the pecan tree," I said. "Too far," people said. "Not for those maniacs," I said.

How could a nice man like Uncle David have such terrible children? This is a question I wish I could answer. Another one is why a nice man like Uncle David would marry Linda Jo's mama. I know that puzzles Mama too. She can't get over how Jeannine left one night, and at that time she was only dating Uncle David. We had a stove going, full of scalded tomatoes. She had been helping Mama can her spaghetti sauce. Helping is not quite the word for Jeannine's standing around practicing that look of hers. All of a sudden, she said she had to take a bath. She was hot and sticky. There stood Mama, stirring the five-gallon blue enamel pans of tomatoes, cooking them down with the fresh oregano she grows herself. There Lee Ann and I stood, wiping off the hot jars that Mama had filled and sealed. It was ten-thirty, but I've known Mama, when she gets to canning, to go on up to midnight. One time, she says, when she had David and Walter picking the tomatoes, she canned all night. If you have them brought to you, the rest is easy.

That's what she says, but it's not really. She just talks that way. I like to hear her make hard things seem easy. I wish she could make this part of our lives easy to live through. But all Mama can see, hear, think, or even dream about is horrible Jeannine and the boys crying themselves to sleep at the Children's Home. They are not crying, I tell her over and over, but she can't hear me. She hates Jeannine. She says she hates herself for not taking in her own brother's children. Then she asks if any normal person would want to take in wild dogs or wild cats? Especially if she already had an epileptic in the house. She's seriously upset when she calls Lee Ann an epileptic.

June 25

...Things are better now. The incident with Lee
Ann's teeth has blown over with everybody but me. I
hardly believe it myself. I'm almost a teenager—one
more year and I'll be thirteen. I already am getting my
period—and I know from all the ads on T.V. about how
depressed and lonely I am going to feel next year
when I am thirteen. For now, let's just say, I only feel
bad when there's a good solid reason—like the thought
of Keith Peller appearing again like he said he would
looking straight at Lee Ann. That thought is worse than
ones about Jeannine, or even Uncle David in the river
or even Lee Ann being taken away.

Looking on the bright side, which is what Angela
tells me to do about stuff at school, I say at least Ms.
Karney can't get Lee Ann without knowing something
terrible about us and then going to a judge and that
would take time.

Angela is one person who knows how to make a
bright side out of the dark one. Her situation and mine
have one thing in common, she points out: we are both
slaves. Me to the Lee Ann thing, and her to her
parents' dream of making a killing over at the lake.
They want to "bring back" the old lake resort, with the
old house called Solitude on the hill above the lake,
and the dance pavilion, turn it into a bed and
breakfast. They have no capital for this venture,

Angela says, so they spend half their time writing grant proposals for government funding for local history projects. She is the one who has to wash the dishes and clean the rooms for the few guests they do have. She is as unfree as I am. At least, she says, my bondage—she loves big words as much as Mama does—has a human side; hers does not. Add to her problem is the fact that her mother is an alcoholic who says she does not have a problem because she recognizes it and if a person recognizes a problem, it is no longer a problem. This kind of thinking is crazy. Look at Keith Peller. I recognize him as a big problem, as evil business, but does he go away? He does not. Angela's mother goes to AA meetings all the time and drinks all the time. I am lucky to live with a binge drinker and a teetotaler mother. Angela says she guesses her mother thinks she comes out even—meetings and drinking—because she is aware of the dangers and on guard. Angela and her mother are biologicals, and it does me good to see the trouble they have. Angela says that when her mother was a girl she would wear only evening clothes, never ordinary school clothes or play clothes or work clothes, never even jeans. Always the organzas and crepe de chines and velvet in the winter. Angela understands her mother's need to always be dressed up so to speak, to refuse to be day-to-day, but that does not mean, she says, that she likes it. She loves to be around Mama, but she does not get to come over that much because of the lake project and all of her responsibilities.

Last year in our Exploratory Latin class, Angela got the whole class to hide in the closet. Twenty-three kids, three deep in the closet along the wall when Old Blue walks in. "Class, class," she said in her dullest voice. Then, she said louder, "People, people, where are you?" We kept dead quiet until she left the room to go get the principal. When he came back with her, there we all were sitting in our seats looking bored. It was wonderful. They shouldn't give such boring classes great names like "Exploratory" anything. We had to do something to perk it up and it was all Angela Marks' idea. Old Blue went on with the class as if nothing had happened. She just said to the principal, "I guess I was wrong." I almost felt bad for her except that she is so boring.

Angela is great on ideas. Her instant solution to the Keith Peller problem was to keep a black snake in our room. Lee Ann does not mind snakes, and Lord knows, I don't. If I did, I would be in the fun house by now, but still that idea is a little too simple. I think a sex maniac, which is what we call Keith Peller though we are kidding in a way, would not stop at a snake, even a humongous one like the ones we have around here. Snake At Window Saves Girl from Stalker. It's too easy. "Won't work," I said.

When Mama starts in on last summer, Walter yells at her asking where does she think he was when David drowned? He knows every blasted g.d. detail of the story. He and David had worked all night the night before on a painting job so they could relax at the picnic. He had wanted to carry David's guitar down to him to play on the river bank because he knew something was bothering him. They hadn't eaten breakfast after the all-nighter, saving up for the fish on the stick or in the pan and the grilled chicken. Who, he yells, does Mama think made that barbecue sauce? Who was with Crystal when she found Lee Ann in the woods when she ran off that day? We all know the answers and he knows we do so it's all right.

June 27

...I'm going to write the way Mama talks. If I don't,
no one would believe it. I can hardly believe it myself.
Since Uncle David drowned, Mama's gotten to be a
talker with one topic—David and Jeannine and things
that connect to them, though Mama can connect most
anything bad to them. Once she said Jeannine was a
communist, but then she took it back because she said
Russians weren't lazy and they weren't dumb and even
communists weren't as bad as we used to think. Then
she said she knew Russians were mean, so...then she
did connect Jeannine to the Russians and the
communists.

She doesn't really care if anybody is there to listen
to her. And Mama's voice and the way she uses her
hands are funny, like she is giving a speech. "Jeannine
rhymes with real mean" she begins, and goes on from
there. "Here she comes when she saw David's new
house he built with Walter to raise those three boys.
She saw some money in it. Sixty-eight thousand taken
away from here in cash. Clear and free as a bird. "And
us living in somebody else's house to fix up for the
third time, since we left Texas where we should have
stayed. David would be alive and he'd be raising his
boys if we had all stayed in Texas. Soon as we got old
man Southall's house fixed, over in Rockview, jacked
up the kitchen and laid a new foundation over the old

rock one, that old fossil came back and told us he was going to have to sell. Walter won't get his house deals down in writing, and I told him that was going to happen, which it did. He'd like to live without writing—shake hands on all deals. What's a handshake to a man like Tom Southall who's getting his old home place fixed for nothing and a good offer comes along? So he shakes with David on building his new house, then fixing us this one twenty miles away from Rockview. I guess our reputation has spread: there are those stupid Texans who'll move into nothing more than a barn and bring it back as a house. But he didn't figure on David's being killed. Killed is what I call it. I'll go on and say—murdered. Anyone who knows, I mean knew David, could tell you that he was friendliness itself and wouldn't hurt a fly. He would work his heart out, but he didn't have a piece of sense about women. The second one that Jeannine thing, made that Mary Louise look like an angel, and I think Mary Louise beat on James Howard until he's foolish in the head. Anybody who slaps a baby crying in his crib should be locked up. I saw Mary Louise do it once. Once was enough. I grabbed her arm and told her she wasn't going to hit her own baby in my house. She said it wasn't my house. He was her baby and she could do what she wanted to him. I said it was more mine than hers, and if she wasn't careful, I was going to turn her in to the Child Abuse people. "Go ahead," she said. "Your word against mine." I squeezed her arm so hard I got down to her bone. Then she yelled, "Okay, Okay." It wasn't too long after that that Mary Louise left.

"I never knew if Mary Louise was stupid or mean or both, and I certainly never knew what she wanted from David—not babies, I know that. She never had a kind word for David or that new house while Walter was working on it at night with David who had gone everywhere in the state on his paint jobs and found all kinds of molding, paneling, staircases, old brick, light fixtures, mantelpieces, flooring, a claw-footed bathtub that held more water than he took to drown. I don't believe he had to buy anything new except the wiring and appliances. He'd roll in at three in the morning, blow the horn, and Walter would jump out the bed and be down the hill to help him unload the panel truck. Crystal would go too if I didn't catch her. Thank God Lee Ann takes a double pill at night or she'd still be in the woods between here and there. It was beautiful for the three months David got to live in his new house by himself—I kept the boys up here at night, but I think they improved from knowing they had their own home, even the baby. Maybe they were glad their mother had gone away. David had set out raspberry and blackberry bushes. He had a ring of rhubarb like we used to have in Ohio before we went to Texas. One time David ran over here from working on his house, on the path he made through the woods. "Make me this pie, Juney Bug," he was yelling. You don't think Mary Louise thought pies got made by human hands, do you? She loved to eat those pies that cost 75 cents out machines, marshmallow dipped in paraffin the color of chocolate. To her, they were pies. She brought Lee Ann one and you'd have thought she'd hung the moon. And Lee Ann has always eaten real food, only she may not know it. That pie David wanted me to make was a rhubarb and strawberry one. If that wasn't strange enough, the recipe from the newspaper in Norfolk, I believe, called for lumps of blue cheese to be crumbled in the bottom of the crust, then the strawberry and rhubarb filling that had been cooked and then chilled. I had to make myself put that blue cheese in the pie, but I have to say, strange tasting as it was, it was good. I'll say delicious. David had brought home railroad ties and terraced him off little sections of garden. He had oregano, basil, thyme, mint and in a damp place, mushrooms. He was getting ready to try to grow some celery where he would have to wrap it up in dirt so's it's the right pale green, almost a white. He had eggplant, had dug an asparagus bed, and all the usual stuff I have. But his garden was in little easy patches and convenient to his back door. He could step outside and pick some plum tomatoes from the two or three staked plants. There was a cucumber barrel that practically handed you a fresh, little cuke. Mine get big and yellow from waiting on me to pick for pickles. They'll have to wait. I can't do it all. David went in the woods and dug up dogwood and ferns to plant around the house down in what you might call a glade. He was talking about starting a mushroom farm on a small scale. For that he needed a pond and pine, I believe, logs for the mushrooms to grow on. It was one of his long-range goals, and I cannot believe he meant to ruin his chances of having his mushrooms by drowning.

"What I wouldn't give to have my own house, not a penny owed on it, my own blood kids, not adopted

69

ones, even seriously disturbed ones like his boys, two of his own and Ernest who is like his own. I wouldn't ever introduce any foreign element to upset the balance.

"Everything was going along just fine when Jeannine came and her friend of some description, Keith Peller. Taking care of Mary Louise and the three kids while the new house went up about killed me. I never knew there was a grown woman who would stay in the bed in the morning and let her baby cry in a dirty diaper, hungry. She did, morning after morning. Walter said it was because she knew I was up at five and would give them something to eat and clean them up. They were like little puppies, begging with their eyes and when I got them clean and decent, they were beautiful and not one thing wrong with them except what she did to them. But all the damage was inside. There was one morning, Mary Louise did gather herself up. The morning she left. That was the one morning she beat me getting up. And quiet! Not one of us heard a sound when she left. She must be part Indian to be that quiet. Maybe she had someone meeting her down at the road, but that's the last we saw of Mary Louise. But like I said, she was an angel compared to Jeannine. When you think about it, Mary Louise was bad to the kids and lazy, but she didn't cause anyone to drown himself. I shouldn't be stuck up here in "rent-free" house that's half killing me and Walter to fix up. This place makes the Rockview place look easy. This one needs more than a foundation. It could use that, plus a roof, and by roof I don't just mean slate shingles which cost an arm and a leg. It needs the roof rebuilt so it can handle the weight. And who is going up on the roof with Walter now, with David gone? I don't know what David thought he was doing when he lay down in the river. You couldn't drown a kitten in that little bit of water. Not knee deep. The boat was practically sitting on the bottom. He had to put his face down to get enough water to drown. It must have been that the thought of what he had got himself into came over him. He must have thought of Jeannine, the papers he had signed, got out the boat, stuck his head under a rock and waited to drown. I know I would. Davey Jr. sucks his thumb until it's raw and James Howard is not right, and Ernest has started wetting the bed and he's eight. Even with Lee Ann, I have to have those boys come back here. Crystal says we need some company, and then she thinks about those boys and takes it back. I don't think I could ever turn my eyes off of them. They burned up one of my bantams. I know they did, not James Howard, he was too busy screaming, but Davey Jr. and Ernest probably thought that was the way to have fun. Dancing around the trash barrel and it was burning good. I ran down there and saw my little bantam thrown sideways on the pile of sticks and leaves, already dead. I saw they had tied his wings so he couldn't fly up. They liked to explode spray cans and it's a wonder they didn't blow off a hand or leg. Sometimes they caught their hair on fire. I thought when I saw my little banty I wished they knew how much fire hurts. Then I remembered they burned themselves as a game. Their arms and legs have scars. I am as sure as I am of anything they will all end up at the State Farm or maybe James Howard will go to a mental hospital. Three ruined children. And a drowned daddy whose house he built and all his work broken down to nothing."

That's the way Mama talks, but I'm tired of writing that way. Think how much energy it takes to talk up a storm like that.

June 28

...You see, that's just how Mama goes on. Now I'm going to say what I want to say here about her talking. No one can stop me, on paper anyway. Mama is wrong to wish for blood-kin babies when she has Lee Ann and me. Yes, it's true, I have wished for my blood mama, but that is natural for children, natural but not serious. Ernest is not blood-kin to Mama as she very well knows, but she loves him anyway, the same as she does Lee Ann and me which is completely or, excuse the word, totally. Once you love someone, you cannot stop. That's her main idea about life. How would Uncle David's boys help her? They might burn the house down if they come here. That's one reason I sometimes want them to. No, I'm kidding. Another reason I would not mind too much their coming is I wouldn't ever be bored and wouldn't have to write down all this family stuff which is enough to make me never want a family of my own, I can tell you.

I will never get pregnant because I am mature and responsible. Look how I take care of Lee Ann, and she's a big fifteen-year-old baby that weighs ninety-eight naked.

If Mama thinks she can keep Lee Ann up here on a bluff in an old house that could fall down any day, keep her out of trouble and everything, she's crazy which is something else I worry about with her. When

Mama goes out to work and leaves us here, there are things that happen that are not exactly trouble-free, if you get what I mean. There's Ms. Karney making visits. I have written down what I think she has in her mind to do. She comes by whenever she's good and ready. And there is Keith Peller who has made his stealth attack.

I don't think Mama is depressed. We have studied depression in teenagers. I don't think you can be so active, talk so much, work so much and still be depressed. I could be wrong. Working hard runs in her family, Mama says. Five o'clock comes, this is in the morning—the day's half gone, she says. It used to kill her the way Mary Louise would sleep till ten-thirty at least. Mama'd bang around, feed the boys, and give them baths making as much noise as she could. Mary Louise was on the fold-out sofa in the living room and Mama would walk through it talking real loud to James Howard. "You poor little baby. You don't have a real Mama to fix you some breakfast. Just trust your old Aunt June."

I walked real heavy upstairs in Lee Ann's room which is over the living room, trying to make Mary Louise get out of bed. I could tell Mary Louise hated us. I think she hated Uncle David by then too, and I believe she hated her own little baby, James Howard. Now he's grown up to be a hateful kid, but back then, he was too little to be hateful. Mary Louise used to say she didn't belong out here in the woods. "Then get in the garden," Mama would yell. "Go pick some snaps." "Why? I don't eat them!" she'd yell back. It was true. At supper, the times when Walter and Uncle David would come in—from working late or getting a load of stuff

74

for the new house—Mama would have the table loaded with fried eggplant, boiled new potatoes and snaps, sliced tomatoes, stuffed peppers, and cucumbers and spring onions. No one he knew of, Walter would say, could get new potatoes and tomatoes on the table at the same time. Tomatoes come in later, July, but Mama got hers in early somehow. What do you think Mary Louise would do? She looked sick staring at the steaming bowls and big platters, saying real fast, "O my lord, O my lord, look at this, look at this!" Then Walter would say the blessing that Mary Louise wouldn't bow her head for, and then he'd say, "Dig in, kids."

Mary Louise would start to the refrigerator and get out her baloney and Miracle Whip. "Who wants a baloney and Miracle Whip?" she'd say as if she were being so generous and sweet.

Naturally, Davey Jr. and Ernest said they did. When Uncle David said, "Let the boys have some real food that June has fixed so nice," she would say, "Onions make Davey Jr. sick and Ernest can't stand anything squishy like that." She was pointing to the fried eggplant.

"This upsets me too much to eat," Mama would say.

"It sure does not show," Mary Louise would say. Mama would get up and leave and that left James Howard in his high chair, me, Lee Ann, Walter and Uncle David to eat. Which we enjoyed. Mary Louise and the two boys ate their sandwiches and then had sugar pops for dessert.

This kind of life lasted a while, but just before Walter and Uncle David got the new house finished enough for them to stay in it, Mary Louise left for good. I guess it would have been harder to leave a new house than to leave an old falling down one with a sister-in-law who had squeezed her arm until the skin broke. This is what I bet Mary Louise told everyone. She had been saying she didn't see the point of building a new house and then ruining it with old stuff—the things Uncle David called his "finds" or "prizes."

At first, I tried to see her point a little, but when I saw how pretty it all looked the way Walter and Uncle David had put it together, I switched over sides to them. I like old and new mixed together. It wasn't a big house, nowhere near as big as this one or Angela's. It was, well, it still is, close to the ground. The windows all look way too big and come to the floor and almost to the ceiling. That's because they're old ones. With all the rocks and ferns, the little squares of garden, it looks like a picture in an old book. I think it looks like a cottage, maybe in England or somewhere. Now strangers own it. They bought it for rental property—that's a hoot. Who would rent a house out here in the middle of nowhere!

TWO

June 30

...When Keith Peller and Jeannine Turner started coming around late last spring, out of nowhere it seemed, but it was really only Lynchburg, and Jeannine ended up married to Uncle David in no time, and we ended up with this terrible new life starring Keith Peller, Mama would cook for them.

It's hard to believe that we "entertained the enemy," but we did. Cooking dinner was Mama's way of giving herself time to take in a situation or, as she says, to clean her gun, call up the auxiliaries, dispatch messengers to the king. It was not hospitality, pure and simple.

"What is?" Mama loves to ask.

Mama seems fiercer than she is. She irons Walter's shirts on the inside and the outside. "So they will feel good inside to him," she says. No one I know does this, and Angela's mom could not believe it. She said it sounded like something out of a fairy tale.

What else does Mama do that belies (she loves that word) her fierceness? When Walter is low (with a hangover) or has a headache, she "bathes his temples" with witch hazel. He says he loves hearing her say those words and she says she loves for him to appreciate her words. That is the story of their love in a nutshell if I had to explain it. Plus, the fact that they adopted Lee Ann and then me which made them even happier.

Mama's feasts, Uncle David called them, did not help us enough. We needed more time and more than time, though time usually helps most things. Mama says that a good meal will sometimes establish a holding pattern, keeping things steady and in place while you consider what can be done.

What she should have done is sprinkle some poison or ground glass in Jeannine's food. And Keith Peller's.

Mama talks in old, high ways. She says her ability to talk comes from not having gone to college with the rest of America, but she can, if and when she wants to, at least talk like a graduate of, say, Susquehanna College. She chooses different colleges for different occasions. She will go on up her scale of talking levels to a university. Temple, SMU, UNLV, Wisconsin, Stanford. She is not afraid of any of them and can talk up a storm.

No, it does not make sense, but it's an education to be around her if you can take it. I am strong and like it. Angela tells me that I should try having a weak mother, even one you love to death—it's much worse than having a strong one. "That makes sense," I tell her. "Thanks a bunch for telling me strong is way better than weak. How did I live without that information?"

I can talk to Angela this way, which is one of the many reasons we are best friends.

"You have done fine without going to college so why are you dead set on it for me?" I ask Mama many times. She does not bother, "deign" she says, to answer.

I am not sure she is right about talking levels and colleges and universities, but I am only twelve, she says, so what do I know, she points out, and I answer that I am Honor Roll since day one, thank you. I test off the charts. She says she would have too if there had been charts and tests when she was twelve.

When I tell Mama that none of my teachers talks the way she does—they do not say flee the city, open a vein, do the unthinkable, turn darkness to day, go to the mountain, sweep the sea away, knit up the raveled sleeve, dip a madeleine, bovarize an ensemble—she says I have poorly prepared, inadequate teachers. Then she adds that dull is nice too, and if I prefer dull to bright, so be it.

When Mama would cook up a storm to give us time to build a fort, so to speak, or whatever she hoped we could do to protect Uncle David from Jeannine and Keith Peller, Jeannine would not get up from the table to fix a bologna sandwich the way Mary Louise used to almost every night, I will give Jeannine that much. But we could tell she didn't like Mama's vegetables or much else about us.

Jeannine was another case of a woman's not being able to resist Uncle David—no one on earth could. It was pure sex appeal which Angela and I have analyzed and analyzed. We have a list of what makes sex appeal. Our criteria, we call it. First, there is the way a boy, or in the case of Uncle David, a man, walks. He has to walk slow as if there were nowhere in particular he wanted to get to. Second, he has to listen to every

81

word and "drink" in your face, I mean look as if he could drink your face down as if it were the sweetest iced tea with lemon and mint in July. Third, he has to laugh easily. He does not have to wear jeans. They help but are not necessary. Uncle David wore painter's coveralls, and they can ruin anyone's appeal. But not his.

Anyway, Jeannine took in with a glance (I often begin to sound like Mama) that we came with the territory. Uncle David thought his sisters, June and Helen, and June's children, Lee Ann (even with her condition, she is sweet and "winning") and of course, me, myself, and I, and Walter were everything people should be. And I am in a separate category of just me, perfect because Uncle David made me feel perfect. His three boys hung the stars, but of course he was blinded by love when he looked at them.

Ernest, for example. Uncle David adopted him as soon as he married Mary Louise and Mama says that Ernest is one of the many terrible reasons for that terrible marriage. She likes to say her brother had to get married as if he had gotten pregnant, that's how much Ernest was Uncle David's own son by the time he and Mary Louise were married. Davey Jr. and James Howard may have been okay as babies, but now they are dangerous, pre-criminals, worse, if that's possible, than when I saw them a year ago, worse because they are stuck off in a foster home or an orphanage, a word no one uses anymore, according to Ms. Karney. Evidently, they shuttle back and forth between the foster homes and the Home (orphanage) because they wear out the fosters so fast.

We use the word "orphanage" because it is a perfectly good word and true, Mama says after Ms. Karney leaves.

Without Uncle David, those boys are doomed to a life of crime, citizens of what Mama calls the nether world of prisons. Her theory about boys is that they need room and freedom to grow in. Girls need, I guess, the opposite. She let the boys build forts with her chairs and blankets in the kitchen in the winter and take all the furniture they could drag outside in the summer. She would cook them "supplies" for their fort and leave them "victuals" wrapped in tin foil and then in big sycamore leaves beside their blanket door. I admit that Lee Ann and I would get in their forts with them and eat what Mama left for us. It was fun in a certain way, I guess. Girls have a different world to live in, Mama would say if asked.

Actually, as Angela loves to say, that was my Uncle David's secret attraction—she means his blindness caused by love. Of course, he loved, in a word, life. So he was blind to life, every big and every little thing. So he loved everything. It's a circle.

To him, all women were beautiful, even Mama, even his two wives. All things were interesting to him. Boring is a word he did not understand. Maybe evil is another.

Angela is going to be a shrink and is practicing on my family. She puts it this way: try being around someone who thinks you are the Eternal Cool, the ultimate number one on the charts, one of a kind, the key stone, the key, the ring, the head honcho, the ne plus ultra (Mama has influenced Angela too) and you

83

will have some small idea of what it was like to have Uncle David around or of what it was that we lost last summer. We lost our winning lottery ticket, Angela says.

Angela has lost only old people so cannot imagine what we have been through. Her grandmother, Gram Holmes, died at eighty-three, but she had been sick for five years and was quite adjusted by the time the end came to the fact that she had to die and soon. Angela has not yet accepted it, but is working on it. Angela was with her when she died because Gram had come to live with them at the lake, and of course, Angela had to do all the work. What made it possible or bearable was Gram Holmes' recognizing that it was Angela who was doing everything, not Gram's own daughter Florence. They had a conspiracy of kindness toward and about Florence, according to Angela. They would not tell Flo for the world that she was not being a good daughter to Gram or a good mother to Angela. They did not want to upset her. Flo is, in some pretty major ways, a jerk, Angela says, but neither she nor her grandmother wanted to point it out, state the obvious. Flo is, to put it another way, "weak" or "fragile" or alcoholic. But Flo has her good points which shine forth, as Angela says, if you are blind to her bad ones.

Uncle David could not see people's bad points, but I guess that is obvious.

Where was Angela's biological dad in this picture? I have asked this question coming out with my secret prejudice about biological parents' being superior in some hard-to-describe way to fosters even if you cannot see it.

Oh, he is just there, is the answer, dreaming his dream of the lake restored to its 1940's heyday with some later stuff thrown in—wild flower walks, a butterfly dome, canoe trips with him in eighteenth century khakis tied up at the knee giving lectures on the one battle that almost happened around here, more of a retreat from an arsenal than a battle. Playing his handmade mandolin. He is writing to movie companies to see if they are interested in a reenactment he would orchestrate. He has the march toward Yorktown and Lee's Retreat down pat and could get our whole school to be extras. He has softened the principal up by coming in for career day and every other kind of day so he looks like a good person, and he is. It's just that he is crazy. Angela's diagnosis again.

Her dad and Flo have the perfect marriage—of two semi-minds, Angela says and laughs hearty-har-har. Then she will tell me the latest crazy thing her parents have done.

The best story most recently was Flo's crying and then announcing that her heart was beating so fast it was going to jump out of her. She prayed out loud—they are very religious—for God to take away some of the heartbeats. There were "too many," she kept saying. God told her to put a record on and dance. So she did. Guy Lombardo slowed her heart down, and she and Angela's dad danced from three-thirty to four-fifteen. Angela watched and then went to report to Gram. They would just shake their heads. "They are the kids; Gram and I were the oldie-goldies," Angela has said over and over.

I tell Angela how much I would like a father who talked. When Mr. Marks comes to school to present historical tableaux, Angela is exasperated (read embarrassed). I tell her, but not much, that I enjoy his talks on Baron von Steuben helping the American troops. She says I don't know what it's like to live with a dreamer dad who is a recovering flower child/pot head, a grandmother who was terminal for years and a flakey mom.

We agree before we get upset that we each have a burden, a different one, a different cross to bear, though she admits that Keith Peller's latest hatefulness of sneaking into Lee Ann's and my room beats what she has to put up with. He's got the mind of a serial killer, she has said, not meaning it exactly, and correcting it to "serial sex offender."

Then we get into one of our favorite conversations: would we rather be raped or killed. I say killed, but Angela argues for rape.

"Let's drive in for a Hardee's," Jeannine said one night, as we sat down to a Brunswick Stew made entirely fresh from the garden. I know because I helped shell the butterbeans after I picked them. Tomatoes, onions, corn, carrots, Gold Rush potatoes—straight from Mama and Walter's garden. I won't mention the potato rolls made with Yellow Finns, light as buttered air.

I think where Jeannine comes from originally, Roanoke Rapids, is the hometown of Hardee's. It's either there or Rocky Mount, I can't remember. Keith Peller wanted to go to town because he was low on beer and he couldn't stand to get low.

Why was he always around is the question. Why was he always attached to Uncle David and Jeannine? That is the question, Mama says, quoting Hamlet as he sat around the castle battlements worrying, as she says he did all in black velvet. She does not have the time Hamlet had on his hands just to sit around talking as if the servants weren't there, she cries.

When I say I do not think Hamlet ever said anything that could be connected to our lives, she says for me to think again. "I'll wait for my senior year to read Hamlet, thank you, so chill," I say, knowing I sound like a mall person who never reads anything except titles of books through store windows, if those.

Jeannine and Mary Louise—Wife Two and Wife One—look a little bit alike if you can believe that anyone would marry the same type of person again and repeat a mistake. Mama says it happens all the time. She goes on about how we repeat ourselves, doing one dumb thing after another. She forgets when she says that that it is her second adopted daughter who is listening.

Jeannine brought to her marriage to Uncle David her sorry excuse for a daughter, Linda Jo Turner, and Mary Louise started out her marriage with Uncle David with Ernest but soon had Davey Jr. and James Howard. It's a blessing that Jeannine did not get herself pregnant—that's the way Mama describes sexual intercourse.

It is always the woman who does it to herself. When I ask Mama why she puts all the responsibility on the girl, something we have discussed as being sad but true in Family Life class, she says men can't help

87

themselves, so women have to be strong. Angela says Mama lives in the dark ages, but is essentially right at least about sex, though evidently sex is not what it used to be when it was secret and in backseats of cars and all the girls either got pregnant or killed themselves worrying or literally.

Uncle David's boys—as I said, he adopted Ernest immediately—have natural propensities for crime. She will give Mary Louise that, meaning that it was genes not Mary Louise by her lonesome who turned the boys into what they are today. Jail Bait.

Both Witch One and Witch Two were, and are still I guess, tiny and had long stringy hair except when they had a new permanent. They dressed alike too. Jeans and high heels. Jeannine started out being nice to Lee Ann and me. She gave Lee Ann her first permanent, but I wouldn't let her give me one. Then she started in about a body wave, and Davey Jr. yelled that anything would help that body. Later he said Lee Ann looked like a wet long-haired cat, but she really looked like a girl on the Ford commercial.

That's when Walter and Mama started fighting again about the operation to tie her tubes, Fallopian, so she couldn't have babies. I have opinions about babies, quite a few.

Mary Louise did not start out being nice to us. She was straight up, I'll give her that. What we saw was what we got.

I have promised myself I would not tell the story of Uncle David's drowning over and over the way Mama does. The way we think about that day reminds me of the hummingbirds Lee Ann thinks we tamed. They stand in the air over the roses and lilacs. Only they're beautiful to see, iridescent blues and greens and blacks. Beads of water under each feather. And of course, the drowning was not beautiful and there was a river, a shallow one, full of water. Just the opposite. One big, flat, mean running color.

When I can't help myself from hovering over the drowning, I make myself concentrate on the little minutes of fun and pleasure we had before everything shattered and the Rescue Squad came. There aren't a lot of those minutes to choose from, because the drowning was not the only terrible thing of the day, even if it was the worst.

Next to the drowning in order of terrible things was the hateful way Keith Peller acted. He came over to my blanket where Lee Ann was stretched out and just beginning to thrash around a little. It looked natural, her thrashing at that point, which was about 12:30. I guess Uncle David had about an hour and a half left to fish.

To live, in other words.

I know some kids at school act like spastics to be funny—if they knew that Lee Ann was one, which they don't because we have kept it a secret and she does not go to school, (the visiting teacher has more or less stopped coming here too—one of the blessings of our situation, Walter says), I know they would walk toward me funny at school, splaying their arms and fingers out like puppets, leaning backwards and bent sideways. I guess it is a little funny when normal people act weird. Sometimes, though, normal people don't have to do anything to look weird. For instance, the way Linda Jo Turner walks would make a dog laugh.

Of course, a dog can't laugh, he can just look sad. Now it is true that a dog can smile some, at least more than a cat who has no facial expressions. You cannot count tilting the head or stretching or rolling. For facial language, you have to look to dogs. We have five dogs because we inherited Uncle David's bird dogs. Big Foot, Useless, Pie, Tigger and Masie. They can do all sorts of things like point at birds you can't even see in ditches and along fences, retrieve dead birds from a long way away, not eat when they are real hungry if you say "Wait a minute, boys." They'll swim out and get dead ducks off the pond and bring them right to you. And the expression on their faces is dead serious. I can't remember all the things they can do. But they have a wide range of feelings that flash across their faces if you pay attention.

Walter says he has never seen dogs so worked out and trained. He said David thought like a dog, which is a compliment coming from Walter. He says animals think better than people, especially dogs, most of them. Soon, I'm going to write down the way Walter talks—when he does talk—which is not all that much, not like Mama, who I have said, can hardly stop herself, and who uses all the phrases she has picked up from her midnight reading sessions which she indulges herself in order to compensate for "not going to Allegheny College."

Lee Ann had on her solid pink sun dress and, after we got up the hill with the cooler of chicken, I could tell she had sneaked back upstairs some way and taken off all of her underwear. I didn't say anything. Fussing won't work with Lee Ann and threatening her doesn't either. Walter and Mama have found that out, a long time ago about both of us, plus they know they can reason things out with me because I am normal.

Keith Peller crawled on his elbows and stomach up to our quilt and put his head down sideways. He could see straight up between Lee Ann's legs. He was drunk so we couldn't exactly tell what it was he was saying. Something about he'd like to see the pills Lee Ann took. He said he was an expert on pills. All the time his head didn't move but was straight like a snake's in the sun.

Lee Ann was twitching herself every which way more and more.

I was trying to carry on a conversation with him but it didn't work. All he wanted to do was stay there, and he was getting an eyeful. I knew that he was after either sex or drugs, not the real thing in either case. I also knew that it would be over my dead body if he got either one. Or a version of either one. I say "sex and drugs" because that is the answer that is always right on any Family Life test at school. In this case though, the drugs were Lee Ann's pills which Keith Peller had an interest in, and the sex was her long beautiful legs and no underpants.

Keith Peller is like a stray dog, looking for scraps of things. He will take what he can get. He has an eye for weakness and gravitates toward it, the opposite of a magnetic field, more of a lost rock from a star hurtling toward some black hole. A star corpse. Yes, Keith Peller is a combo of stray dog and dead star. And snake, I forgot the snake. That sums him up perfectly. He dresses like a rock-star cowboy. But he is, we think, a hairdresser, motel maintenance man though no one has ever seen him working.

What cannot be summed up even imperfectly is why he came into our lives or why we let him. Until that day at the picnic, he had never been so upfront with his moves on Lee Ann, if you don't count his trashy talk. But that day of the picnic when Uncle David would lie down in the river and drown, Keith Peller seemed different, determined to do something more evil than just be his slime-ball self.

Davey Jr. and Ernest were swimming in the river. James Howard was down there too. He's four now, but even when he was just three and had a family, no one watched him because it did not do any good. If his brothers were swimming in the river, James Howard was too. If they were burning branches, he was. I will say that no one on earth, probably not angels or devils either, could have stopped James Howard from following his brothers to the river, and why he has not drowned or burned himself up is a question maybe God knows the answer to.

James Howard is the one who should have drowned that day.

If James Howard had been the one the Rescue Squad had driven off with, Uncle David would have carried on and dedicated his life to bringing loads of inner city kids out to live with us in the summer or maybe all year round in memory of James Howard. That part would have been terrible, but in the long run, I will have to say, it would have been better for

James Howard to have fallen in the river face down and floated away until someone fished him out.

Of course, James Howard can swim and climb rocks and he would never have drowned. Three days later he would have walked into the sheriff's office and given him our phone number which Mama had made him memorize so he could call her if he ever needed his Juney Bug. At three, last summer, James Howard was in fact about eight years old because of his rough child or babyhood.

The river was so low, shallow there at that spot where they were mainly playing on the rocks and jumping out on old vines. They didn't care if they hit the rocks. In fact, the rocks made it interesting. A river by itself did not mean much to them.

Uncle David thought that it was good to jump on rocks in a river, very good. The higher the better. He never thought about falling or breaking anything. Those ideas never occurred to him.

Jeannine was hoping, I bet, that they would split their heads on the rocks. Mama knew that they shouldn't be jumping out on the rocks but she also knew she could not stop them.

Walter probably should have adopted him some boy babies if there had been any available instead of you know who and you know who—me and Lee Ann.

Jeannine's precious Linda Jo was back at the house under her standing hair dryer. Her room looked like a beauty parlor. She took over James Howard's room and he had to move in with the big boys. It took Linda Jo two hours to get ready to leave to go anywhere. Losing his room is one of the many things wrong with

James Howard. Angela says he was a displaced person in his own home. Now he's in an orphanage or foster home, we are not sure. "Where do you think we're going," I asked Linda Jo. Then I answered "A PICNIC!" because I knew she was too dumb to think of anything. She calls what she is "bored."

How could she have been bored with a picnic like the one we were having? The fish caught right there, the slaw made from the humongous Scarlet O'Hara cabbages Walter grows and then Mama adds itty-bitty pieces of her orange peppers to make it pretty and very hot, Mama's light bread and her five-layer applesauce cake with lemon icing. A grass sliding board down to a river, the water that clear brown, and fish twitching around the rocks. Grapevines—everything.

What would you call it? Not "boring," if you are any smarter than Miss Turner and have any talent for vocabulary.

"We're going up the hill, up on the river bluff, that's all, just us. You don't need to be fixing up your hair to go. The wind's going to tear it to pieces anyway and maybe off your head." This is what I said to Linda Jo, trying to help her.

I added, "I hope," thinking she'd get from under the hair dryer, but I was wrong. She is a throwback, a recessive gene or something. No one sits under hair dryers except old women in beauty parlors. I guess Keith Peller got her doing it.

This summer in her fits, Mama's talking to herself. "June," she will say, "don't you think it's odd that Keith Peller went down to the river when he knew the boys were playing on the rocks down there, though upriver? That man who could not stand to be around those boys? That man who must have watched David lie down in the river? Why did Keith Peller go at just that time, just then? What did he say to my David?" Then Mama answers herself, "I can figure some of the things he could have said such as, "I'm getting me some, as much as I want, from your little wife." I don't think they ever stopped, maybe a day or two for the wedding. And of course, now that David is gone, they don't have to sneak around. They can do it any time they so please."

I think I'll use the short word "whir"—the sound a hummingbird's wings make, to show I'm standing over, whirring over the day at the river again. The part of the day with Keith Peller in it gets a little mixed up. So much was happening, but we didn't, not one of us, understand what was actually happening? I don't think so, anyway. Maybe we won't ever.

Whir.

"Where's your pretty, crazy sister's pills?" Keith Peller asks me. "None of your beeswax," I say.

That's when he put his fingers around my ankle, never taking his eyes off Lee Ann's you know where, and began squeezing. I could feel the gristle or whatever that cord is in your ankle begin to go flat against my leg bone. I remembered Mama squeezing Mary Louise's arm for slapping little James Howard in his crib, and I know how strong Mama is and what marks she made on Mary Louise's arm.

Whir.

Keith Peller could have broken my ankle just with his fingers which were all beauty parlor soft, perfect cuticles. Uncle David never had paint on his hands even after painting all day. So I tried to hide the Rexall bottle I carry in my pocket every day when I'm not at school. There were three tablets left in there from the five we started with in the morning after breakfast. Mama had counted out five that morning as usual and I was in charge of Lee Ann's pills, as usual.

Except for the horrible ending of the picnic, Mama would have taken my skin off if I had been a pill short at bedtime, but because Uncle David had been taken away by the rescue squad but not to the hospital, just to the funeral home, she never noticed the pills.

Later, when Walter and I brought Lee Ann home out of the woods that night, Mama didn't notice where the bedtime pills came from. Right under her nose, I got two out of the big bottle in the cabinet over the stove to make up for the one Keith Peller stole just before he went down to talk to Uncle David.

I had been so glad that I could stand up on my leg and that my ankle hadn't been broken in his grip, I didn't take in until that night that one pill was gone, and that the bottle must have slipped out of my pocket. Lee Ann needs two pills to get through the night, but we always get the extra one out of the big bottle. I don't know why we do. I bet when he slid the bottle in front of his nose and read the label, drunk as he was, he started smiling like a joke was glued on the bottle instead of her prescription.

I know it's dangerous for normal people to get any of Lee Ann's medicine in them. Mama and I had to go to a special class on medications for epileptics, what to eat with the pills, how to be careful no one but the person who "is subject to seizures" is given the drug. We stayed a whole day for it. I wasn't the only kid there. The nurse who talked said children were often "caretakers." I could have told her an earful about that, but I kept my mouth shut.

Whir.

Keith Peller looked terrible even though he was laughing when he let go my ankle, flipped over on his back and began laughing harder, a dark, dirty laugh. That must have been when the pill bottle got away from my pocket.

"Run get your Uncle Keith a beer out your Mama's cooler." "You ain't my uncle. I am adopted," I said. I used "ain't" because I was talking to him. Bad English for bad people.

"Then run get your boyfriend a beer," he said.

"You certainly ain't any boyfriend of mine."

"Look," he said, all of a sudden sitting up and mad as a snake about something. "Then, I'll be your crazy sister's boyfriend. I could do her some good. She's begging for one."

"You ain't any kind of friend of any kind on earth to my sister or me." I yelled this as I was running away.

That's what we said to each other in the last conversation we ever had—not counting when I yelled in a whisper for him that night when the house was in an uproar to get out of our room or I would get Walter who would shoot him. That's when I got Lee Ann out of our room and standing by the stairs and then, as I have said once, I encouraged her to fall down the steps.

97

Would she rather be raped or have her teeth broken was what I asked myself. The answer was obvious.

I have been glad since last summer that I got the last word in with Keith Peller, that I said he was a big nothing to me and Lee Ann, but I like what I said about Walter shooting him too. He left before Uncle David's funeral. The next-to-last last time we had seen him was when he showed up in our room the evening of the picnic-drowning.

So that's a pleasant minute of the picnic-drowning day to remember—when I told Keith Peller off—even if it is all mixed up with terrible things. The best minute is when I thought of making Lee Ann fall down the steps and was able almost immediately to bring it off.

I might tell Mama about Keith Peller's stealing the pill, I mean, that I think he stole it. I am sure that he took it himself as a drug-drug, not to try to sell. The nurse told us that on the street, which around here means in one of the twenty or thirty deserted houses, the pills would bring a lot of money because in normal people, who don't have brain disorders, the pills make them high. She said "will give an incredible high." She said beware of pushers knowing you had the medication. To them it meant a great deal of money. It was speed, local speed.

We didn't pay much attention to that part of the nurse's talk at first, but Angela, who knows a lot about everything, especially the dark side of things, says that part was the key to what the nurse was saying and the key to the Peller mystery; we do not have to wait until we get to the high school to learn about drugs even though we are out in the country, the capital of nowhere, we call it. It'll be a different world in high school, but not really that much as far as drugs go.

That's exactly what the word means in high school. HIGH. That's what Angela claims is a fact. She says drugs are everywhere in high school. They are almost everywhere in our school which is a combination elementary and middle because the real middle school burned down last year. Set on fire by Duane Mitchell after he had been given his third ISS, and after the third, you are out for the year. He told everyone he couldn't go home because bad as school was, it was better than the home show, so he went on his lunch period to the Stop N' Shop and got a milk jug of gasoline and poured it all around the computer room for later that night.

Angela says you can get local speed, and it's pretty easy.

Whir.

July 4

...If I did tell Mama about the missing pill, I know she'd be much worse off knowing than she is not knowing. If she thought Keith Peller stole a pill from Lee Ann's bottle, went down and talked to Uncle David, came right back up, almost pulling up the paw paw trees as he grabbed them, then jumped in his van drunk as a skunk with Jeannine and took off, Mama would go crazy, and she is half crazy now. Hearing that, she would be entirely crazy if she knew Keith Peller was looking up Lee Ann's legs.

When the rescue people got Uncle David up the hill, they couldn't believe he was dead because they all knew he could swim, the water wasn't even deep enough to have his boat in it, and he didn't look like he'd drowned. They didn't know exactly why, but he didn't look just dead from drowning.

"Maybe he's not dead!" That's what I screamed. I know from T.V. that you can breathe into almost dead people and bring them back. Mama was trying to give him a chance to come back.

"No, he's dead as's possible," the head person said. "Can't be deader," I remember one of them saying.

This was when, actually, I guess it was a little later, that we noticed Lee Ann had gone off in the woods. Summer woods are bad in Virginia. There are snakes, chiggers, ticks, poison oak—you name it. But they don't worry Mama so much as the possibility of Lee Ann's getting herself so far off we can't find her and she'll go into a spasm and get tangled up in briars.

Whir.

Davey Jr. sits down by his daddy who is wrapped up like a log in Mama's quilt and sucks his thumb. They don't move Uncle David until Jeannine comes back. A wife is more important than a sister.

Everyone just sat around on the blankets being very quiet. This summer as Mama goes over and over that day (it looks as if I'm doing the same thing myself) she says they took their own sweet time getting back, Jeannine and Keith Peller.

"June," she says, "think about it: a drunk man and a poor excuse for a woman gone off in a van with pictures painted on the sides. What do you think?"

"It's no good," is her answer to herself.

I'm just glad he took Jeannine off with him instead of Lee Ann which is what he wanted to do. I know more about sex than I would like to, more about the bad side of it than about the good side of it, if there is one.

Lee Ann was better off out in the woods than in his van, which is exactly why I had to trick her into walking into the woods. She loves to ride in vans and has gone a few times with Walter to work when he was driving one he had borrowed. I love vans too.

Once she and I got into Keith Peller's van—he was sleeping off a drunk so we were safe. In the back there is a water bed that takes up all the floor. There were cabinets with snacks and whiskey. It was set up very nice, I mean I was surprised a person like Keith Peller could fix up such an interesting van. He had a built-in stereo and fur, not real fur, on the walls and floor. Walter was working on his house, and Keith Peller was working on his van. I have seen him take all day one Sunday to wax it.

If Mama gets better, any better at all, I may tell her about the pill I'm sure Keith Peller stole. If she gets well, I may tell her that he got in the house, not through the door. I have never lost a pill, I've never even spilled one. Mama says or used to say that I could grow up to own and operate a drug store and that there is more to them than used to be. Now we buy shoes at the Rexall where we get Lee Ann's prescription filled. You can buy tires, wine, lawn chairs, almost anything in the world. Walter says anything that is worthless and you don't really need you can buy at a Super Drug.

This will be easy to write down—the way Walter talks—because he doesn't that much. I guess there's not all that much to talk about. Mama does the talking about big things like Uncle David, of course, his boys coming here to live, the day at the river, the evil Jeannine and the more evil if possible, Keith Peller.

Walter doesn't like football or stock car racing, the things men can really talk up. Angela's dad, he likes regular things like that. But Walter likes hunting-- that's pretty regular, but by hunting, I mean just walking through the woods early in the morning. He doesn't carry a gun all the time and Mama swears he's going to get shot himself one morning by the fool turkey hunters. They go out at sunrise and hide. They shoot at sounds, not what they see.

Mama is waiting for Walter to come home dead. You'll get yourself killed and leave me with these girls to raise. Then he'll say, if he's in the mood, that she would feel better when he's shot dead if Lee Ann had had her operation so she can't have babies. He gets mad when he sees deer flopped on the roof of cars, their long necks curving down over the windshield. Who could kill a little thing like that, he always says. Not that they are little, some of them almost cover the windshield, at least on the little cars.

He's never shot anything. Once he hit a deer that jumped out at his truck and we got us a freezer full of venison. His truck was in the shop for a month and he had to ride to work with Uncle David.

I think that's when they got to be even better than best friends. They had a job over in Lynchburg which is two hours away. Sometimes they had to get a motel and spend the night, sometimes they worked all night.

According to Mama, they planned to go into the painting business together, only it was going to be more than just painting. Fixing up old houses (Walter sure knows enough about that kind of stupid work), building decks and swimming pools at housing developments, making new driveways that swoop up close to your front door.

"Total Homes" was going to be the name of their business. All that is ruined now, but Mama says it was ruined before Uncle David got himself drowned. That's what she calls it.

She's beginning to think that something was wrong with the plans for "Total Homes," something to do with Jeannine. "Money and sex," she says, then

103

reverses it to "sex and money." It was at the Day's Rest Motel that Jeannine and Keith Peller got into our lives. She worked at the motel desk. She claimed she was a computer expert, but Mama says she just watched a little screen that never changed. It had the prices of everything on it. I don't know the truth.

Keith Peller was the manager (maintenance-man, beauty operator, whatever) at the motel where the beauty parlor, which was just a room, was down the corridor from the front desk. We did not know he cut hair. But what we did not know could fill a book, and is...get it?

Anyway, he got himself invited down "in the country" to our house for a weekend. It wasn't long before Jeannine was coming too. It wasn't long after that, that we had us a wedding to give, but not for Keith Peller and Jeannine Turner.

At the time, being so relieved that Mary Louise had gone off somewhere, we didn't know where or care, we were glad, downright happy to have a wedding to work on. "Short sighted in the long run," Mama says now.

"Well, June," Uncle David said then, "just because you are dragged down by this old worthless man named Walter from Ohio, Walter, doesn't mean your little brother can't be happy. The boys need a Mama, like your girls have you."

"You can't figure that little thing that's mostly hair, the one with that daughter that lives on soft drinks and Twinkies, is going to be a Mama to anyone."

This talk went on before and after the wedding.

You get tired of venison real fast, I can tell you. It tastes something like the woods, like you think woods tasted if you could take a bite of them. Strong and sharp. Mama says it is the taste of the wild. Walter says he likes it better than corn-fed hogs and heifers that were so fat they couldn't walk. He might not shoot deer, but once they are dead, he can't see a thing wrong with eating them. In fact, he thinks all the shot-up deer should be eaten, but he bets most of them end up in a landfill somewhere.

But every bite I took tasted for the world like a deer jumping out at a car in the dusk and smearing blood and hair all over the windshield. My mouth kind of lifted up over barb wire from the taste.

In Texas, you eat steak or steak burgers. Aunt Helen brought us some in a cooler when she came for the funeral, frozen hard as rocks, and her own barbecue sauce.

Mama, and I think Walter too, see this place (rent-free) as THE HOMEPLACE. They've started calling it that, which makes me sick because they'll start believing themselves if they don't watch out and that will be the end of going back to Texas, as a family I mean.

I just might really have to pack up Lee Ann and me and find us a way back to Texas and start a new life with Aunt Helen, or at least take a vacation from the trouble here. The Greyhound won't even stop near here anymore. I have heard the closest stop is Keysville which is at least twenty miles away. Why should it, Walter said, when everybody had his own truck or car or both. He says Ohio where he grew up is something like Virginia. I say poor Ohio. He says no, Ohio has the same high river bluffs hanging over narrow little rivers in the part he knew.

I keep my trap shut and don't say, "But nobody goes and drowns in the little rivers, no bigger than creeks I bet, like in some states."

To Walter, Texas was ugly, big and flat. He was glad to get to a place like Sandys Point with hills and curvy roads where you never know what's coming.

Since Walter keeps his thoughts to himself, I think I'll just make up what it looks like to me he is thinking. I don't believe Mama knows what goes on inside his head either. I listen hard to hear them talking, but they don't, except if you count fighting. They can pitch a fit now and then—over taking in Uncle David's boys, for one. They are both for taking the boys, but they fight about it anyway. The details. Walter wonders, and I think he is right, whether it will work out. Once children get away, it's hard to get them back, he says. Whether Jeannine and Keith would ever come back here was another knock-down, drag-out. They were both on the same side—it would be hell to have them within a thousand miles, much less next door, but I guess it's a possibility. That makes it look more and more like Uncle David's boys will be coming to live here, so it also is looking like I better make plans to leave, at least go visit Aunt Helen and hope that she invites us to live with her in Texas as I am sure she will once she sees how happy she is to have us with her full time. I think I would go crazy, crack up forever, if I had to stay here and put up with Uncle David's boys and Keith Peller. I know that they have to come here. It's their last and only chance to be saved from lives of crime. I know they are miserable, very sad to be in their foster homes or the Home, but I know I will lose it if they do come here, not to mention Keith Peller and his habit of roaming into houses where a girl named Lee Ann is sleeping.

I will miss Angela, but she can come visit us in Texas.

Two big things to do: Number one is save up Lee Ann's medicine. Number two is get some money. We need to ride on the bus, not hitchhike. Saving my lunch money when school starts will give me 9.25 every week. By Christmas, I'll have enough to get halfway to Texas, probably to Kentucky where I don't know a living soul. But 45.50 will get just me that far. I called Keysville and asked. It would buy two tickets to Bristol, Virginia, or Tennessee. "That's a joke, the woman on the phone said. Why? I said. Because Bristol, Virginia, and Bristol, Tennessee, mean the same thing, Honey." I said back, "Whatever, Sweetie."

I know Bristol, either one, is not close enough to Texas to be worth going to. If Mama would let me take money for doing the jobs I do for the old women she works for, I could start saving up sooner than from lunch money, but oh no, she says, senile as Mrs. Jamison and Mrs. Harris are, the one thing they don't get mixed up on is money matters and young people, and she thinks that it is not good to pay children for helping because then they expect to be paid for doing what they should do. She says sweeping the porch or feeding the birds or any of the dumb little jobs they always want done right away are easy for me to do and do gladly without recompense. I should learn the joy of doing and giving.

I wish we lived in a trailer, nice and neat with fold-up, hidden beds and ironing boards, little T.V.'s stuck back in a cabinet. Then we would not have room for Uncle David's boys. It's clear that I must do something much worse than run away to Bristol.

Mama tells me I look like a hornet in the face when I get mad. I don't really, I look like the singer on Kids World who has hair as dark as mine and eyes almost as brown. I know I am pretty, for my age, and will probably turn out to be beautiful and marry a rich man. I won't do what my real Mama did—think I am in love. I won't do what my Uncle David did—get tangled up with the worst two people on earth. Mary Louise, the Mean, and Jeannine, the MEANER.

Whir.

I wonder why people are mean. They just are, Mama says, for no reason. She and Walter agree that animals are better than people. But some animals are mean, I say. Not really, they say. As far as I can tell, Uncle David and his boys, this animal thing and this rent-free wrecked-up house are what Mama and Walter have in common. He wants her to take Uncle David's boys. She says she will in a minute if he'll help her convince Ms. Karney that we are an alcohol-free environment. He admits that will be hard. With sleeping all day, he wouldn't have the trouble of the boys, he admits. Walter's great appeal, Mama says and I agree, is that he tells the truth, like it or not, live or die, hell or high water, he'll lay it on the line.

Oh no, he says. He knows he would just have the fun of them, and for him fun and hell are first cousins. He says Crystal Ball will help with the boys. I am glad that Mama is also honest enough to say Crystal Ball has her work cut out for her with Lee Ann.

I am glad I have two honest parents and glad that I have planned our itinerary as far as Bristol, Virginia, and Tennessee at least. And even Mama doesn't know how hard that work to take care of Lee Ann is. She still doesn't know how terrible Keith Peller was to Lee Ann and that he is the real reason she ran off in the woods—the real reason I made her run away—the day Uncle David drowned. Or, the real reason she "fell" down the steps.

Everyone thought she ran away because she saw Uncle David's dead face, and that was part of it, but the biggest reason was the hateful way Keith acted, looking up between her legs. I know murder, which is what Mama claims was done that day, is much worse. But at the time, we never thought of anybody being murdered. And not for a long time after. Words can't murder anyone, and all Keith Peller did down at the river—that we know of—was talk to Uncle David just before he got out of the boat and lay on the bottom of the river. Good people are always dumber than evil people. I don't know why, but it's true.

Look at me. I don't mean to brag, but think I am a good person. I work at it. Many times, I do not hit Lee Ann when I certainly could. No one is there to see. But being good, or mostly good, makes me dumb.

I know from Health and Community class that there are many kinds of intimidation. Oh no, my friends, you people reading this when I am D___ and G___, my real life will start when I get us to Texas, all of us, James Howard, Davey Jr. and Ernest, Mama and Walter, Lee Ann, me and Angela. She can bring her parents if they are in any condition, mentally speaking, to come. It will take years to accomplish these things, as Mama would say.

Okay, it doesn't have to be every single one of us. It can be some of us. Leave out the boys, even leave out Mama and Walter. They don't want to leave Sandys Point anyway. They would be very unhappy away from here. And maybe even Angela and her parents.

"Basically," as Angela loves to say, the two people who have got to leave here are Lee Ann and her brilliant sister. For one thing, I can't leave Lee Ann here with Keith Peller hanging around, sneaking into our room.

July 6

...Angela's breasts were like small August tea roses, flattened in the way rose petals are, the white ones about to bruise in the heat. Mine were flat as leaves.

Miracle of miracles, I got to spend the night with Angela without Lee Ann.

We were looking at our naked reflections in the wavery window, trying a kind of therapy Angela had seen on television.

It was to help people understand themselves. "Right, if they can stop laughing long enough," she said.

"This doesn't work with just anybody, and of course, it's better with women. Girls don't have much to show, but we are old for our ages, we have breasts, at least I do, and you almost do. Lee Ann would be best as far as being naked goes, but she doesn't talk. Now, you tell the truth; you get to go first. That's the theory. Nothing to hide. Two naked people staring at themselves. We are supposed to have a full-length mirror but we don't, so a window will do. We are now in session: you tell the truth and then I tell the truth and we have to agree to anything we want to talk about. The man on T.V. said agree to anything but sex and money. Ha Ha. He thought he was so funny."

"We already know the truth about each other, don't we? I hate to ask a stupid question." I didn't hate to at all but said I did.

"We think we know the truth, dumb face, but we don't. Because the truth is harder to know than people realize."

Angela thought that we could deal with things better—the Keith Peller problem, her parents and their on-going soap opera, Lee Ann, Uncle David's death, the possibility of Ernest, Davey Jr. and James Howard all moving back home with us, if we tried this weird self-help thing. She looked happy, and I was so glad to be there, I did not care what we did. It could be this or go out on the lake in the old row boat we had found sunk and rescued and cleaned up for our excursions and adventures. Pack a lunch, get our fishing gear, and we were in heaven for a few hours. But because I got to come over only once every twenty years, I was surprised at this substitute fun, this "new kind of fun," Angela called it.

She got us the bottles of warm beer she had been saving under her bed for when I could come over. She had expected it to be in thirty years, so she just had two bottles each. Her dad was always around, so it was hard to get. We wanted to be sure that we hated beer, and there was only one way to be sure. Deprive us.

So, we were at the lake that would soon be on the historic tour map, if Angela's father's letters and petitions work, in Angela's old house that looks down on the lake, soon to have an old paddle-wheel steam boat to take the tourists around. We drank ten swallows of beer each, put on our clothes and lay down to die laughing at the thoughts of people on the boat looking at trees and sky and then sky and trees. "Don't forget the lake! They have the water to look at!"

Angela loves her own jokes and if she has a fault, this would be it. She added that tourists could hear the story of the house being moved on logs up the hill to look down over the lake, the house that was once a tavern, "and still is, for some of us" Angela said raising her beer bottle, called "Solitude."

I love the name "Solitude" as much as I love "Dead and Gone." The fallen plaster, exposed laths in the ruined walls of the front rooms, the gutters added during Eisenhower's presidency pointing down like long fingernails, the sagging shutters and chimneys drifting away from the house were like ours at home only older, there were more things falling apart, more of everything, and much grander. Angela's parents wanted to live in one room in the back with a microwave and television while they renovated the rest of the house, but Angela and Gram forced them to fix it up a little bit more. As she said, "creature comforts" like electricity and plumbing which were just barely "up to code" now, and Angela had a big down comforter that had a meadow of pink and green flowers on it. This was her central heating.

They put heat in Gram's room, but nowhere else. Wood stoves, authentic as anything, Angela said, everywhere else. It was pitiable and ridiculous to see her parents gathering sticks like hermits to burn in those stoves.

One year at Christmas they ordered a whole load of wood, and that was the warmest they had ever been. The wood yard at Sandys Point delivered wood cut to the length you wanted, but you had to want it and write a good check for it, Angela pointed out.

We lived six miles away from "Solitude" but it could have been sixty. Sandys Point was between us.

"Okay," I told her, "I will go first and tell this truth which is a question: I want to know if I am right about not telling anyone but you about Keith Peller."

"That's easy. Simple. Absolutely, silence is key here. If you tell your Mama, she will go off and then Ms. Karney will really get on your case, and you will, just as you have said, lose Lee Ann along with the possibility of getting the boys, which, of course, is a good thing in my mind. Let's get on with other things."

THREE

July 20

...You won't believe this, whoever has found my book! I am rich. I have four hundred dollars in my little jewelry box. No, I did not steal it the way I thought I would have to. What is better, I have found us a way, an easier way than the get-on-the-bus-at-Keysville-way to Texas. Well, let's say, I have found a way toward Texas, to the edge of Virginia anyway. To Danville, where Camp Independence is and where people like Lee Ann go to learn how to live with other handicaps, which is the word kids at school use for people like Lee Ann.

I will go with her. I don't know if I will be the only normal person there, but as I told myself—a joke and not that funny—I am used to that situation.

Danville is at least closer to Texas and Aunt Helen than this godforsaken place where Keith Peller may show up at any time day or night, and I think that he has actually come here once or twice in the flesh again. There are signs—tire tracks that don't match Walter's or Mama's or Ms. Karney's, his big tires, and the phone calls that come with no one at the other end. Heavy breathing like kids at school do, but he doesn't laugh the way they do when they call.

Godforsaken is what Mary Louise called Sandys Point, and Jeannine would have too if she had such a word in her vocabulary. She used to say "godawful" a lot and other worse words which I will record all in one place in this book so they ruin just that part.

Ms. Karney got money for Lee Ann to go to camp from the Woman's Club, and then when Mama said Lee Ann couldn't go without Crystal Ball, Ms. Karney coughed up the money for my way too. She probably had to claim that I was a handicap or retarded. Nothing that woman does surprises me.

More and more it has been looking like those awful boys, my cousins by adoption, poor Uncle David's kids, are really coming to live with us. And of course, part of me is glad, and the other part is the opposite. Ms. Karney, again, is doing her thing with papers. She claims that Davey Jr. has been "severely beaten" by his foster dad who had Davey Jr. by himself just three weeks. I said to myself that I did not entirely blame the foster dad and that three weeks was not that long and that maybe another few weeks would iron out the wrinkles.

We want them to come and we don't want them to come. Angela says we are deeply ambivalent. Truer words were never spoken.

So I am going with Lee Ann to camp. I will have twenty-four days' worth of pills for Lee Ann, I will have the four hundred dollars that I was given by Mrs. Jamison, the old woman Mama worked for last week and has for some time.

My plan is simple: go to the camp, check out the buses from Danville to Houston, pack up some camp food, sweet talk us a ride to the bus station, and bingo, leave Virginia and hit the highway back to Aunt Helen, Texas and our real home. What happens when I get us

118

to Houston will have to wait for me to plan on the bus because I do not have time to think about that part now. I will write a letter to tell Angela my plan only after I get to camp because she might feel she has to tell someone, not ratting on us, but exercising mature judgment, she would call it. I will not tell Aunt Helen until we get to Houston for the exact same reason. Talk about deeply ambivalent. That is what she will definitely feel when she hears my voice from the Houston bus station which, I bet, is in a bad part of the city if it is like the one in Richmond. But, basically, she will be happy to see us. I will tell her about Keith Peller on one condition—one I have not thought of yet, but I know it had better be a good one. Maybe she will see that if she tells Mama about him, Mama will feel that she has to go to the sheriff because she already thinks that it was Keith Peller who helped Uncle David drown, that is, killed him, and that she should have talked to the sheriff about that long before. If Mama knows about Keith Peller's plans for Lee Ann—sex at some level—she will go crazy, go to the sheriff and that will be all that Ms. Karney needs to write up her report that our home is not a "nurturing environment" for Lee Ann or Uncle David's boys. Me, I guess, no one worries about having a safe environment. I admit I don't either.

So forget me in all this concern about nurturing. I guess Mama will think that Crystal Ball can take care of herself. I agree.

How I got the money is this: Mrs. Jamison is sitting at her big window that comes all the way down to the floor. Lee Ann is stretched out on the long needle

119

point sofa which has faded roses and castles in blocks on it. This is what she does when she goes with us to Mrs. J's. Mama is outside washing the big window with vinegar and newspapers balled up. I am doing the inside panes. The sunshine is crackling against the shining glass.

"Such luxury," old Mrs. J. says. That's one of her favorite things to say about sunshine or any little thing. Then, out of the blue, she tells me she wants to give Lee Ann and me a "little something" for our camp trip. Mama can't hear us through the window. Mrs. J. sends me into her bedroom, which is big enough for a whole camp to live in, and tells me to look in her top bureau drawer, which I do, of course, and find, voila, the envelope marked Crystal Annette Ball and Lee Ann Ball!

Isn't that a sign that I am doing the right thing with this Houston plan? I give her a kiss when I come back, the envelope carefully folded and deep in my jean's pocket.

"Don't tell your Mama," she says, and I pat her which makes her make her one joke to me, "Don't pet me. I'm not a dog."

"Oh, no," I say back.

Mama cannot tell what is going on through the window. It looked as if, I guess, I were just being thoughtful and considerate and doing little jobs for Mrs. J., running into her bedroom, running back, the way people love for kids to do.

I have told Lee Ann we were going to meet our real mothers in a Houston, Texas, restaurant. We will drink cokes with them and then call back up here to Walter

120

and Mama to tell them we are okay. I will have our telephone credit card, I am sure, because Mama will want me to have it at camp to call her every night.

These lies about our mothers and the restaurant are necessary. We are really going to our Aunt Helen's, of course, but I cannot say this or Lee Ann will want to leave yesterday. Aunt Helen cannot know we are coming. As I said, I cannot trust her not to exercise her mature judgment and get right on the phone to Virginia and her baby sister June. Juney-Bug and The Baby were her world, she loves to say, laughing at things she remembers about her childhood with Mama and Uncle David, and then she will be crying over Uncle David.

Lee Ann repeated, in her way of talking, everything I had acted out or "pictured" for her about going to Texas. Happy is not the word for how she felt when I told her what our plan was. The way I talk to Lee Ann is unusual. I am developing a new kind of language called "picturing," Mama says.

Lee Ann did not understand the plan in the right order, but I was sure that she knew we were leaving for Aunt Helen's in Texas. Because the camp idea was attached to the Texas plan, it was a little hard for her to understand, plus she is hopeless about time in the future. I did not try to picture the time part, August first, the day we leave. But she did her best to get the picture that she was not really going to have to learn to swim—that was the main point—at Camp Independence. Ms. Karney thought that swimming was one of the main reasons we were going, and Mama and Walter thought so too. I can imagine why

121

swimming was a big thing in their minds for us in spite of the fact that it took only a few feet of water for Uncle David to drown in and he could swim like a fish. But nothing makes sense when people are brokenhearted.

Lee Ann has a very large residual vocabulary, Mama says, a silent one, so she can understand oceans. Time and deception are two abstractions that I have not figured out how to talk about to Lee Ann, so I don't, but I can do hatred and fear really great. Lee Ann knows we hate Keith Peller, that she should be afraid of him. It was hard to convince her because he had started out as Uncle David's friend and he got stuck in her mind as that.

I know Keith Peller is counting on that to get Lee Ann in a place she may not be able to get out of. That is, where I am not, though where would that be? I cannot even imagine being in a place where Lee Ann was not, except over at Angela's once every twenty or thirty years for one night.

It was impossible to picture to Lee Ann what was really going to happen and how that was different from what people thought was going to happen: we would be at this camp for a day or two—not swimming—but then we would leave for Texas. It's hard for me to believe it, and I am the one who has to carry the plan out.

I was counting on the fact that no one would know we were missing until we are deep into Kentucky at least. My ideas about camps are limited, but I don't think they lock people up at night or at rest times.

Seeing a white moth when I took Lee Ann out for a walk around Mrs. J's boxwoods that have little gravel paths between them and Lee Ann loves to be "lost" in for a few minutes helped me picture our Texas trip. Lee Ann loved for me to pop out and surprise her, as if I had not been only two feet away. The white moth trapped in the boxwoods helped her understand the plan for Texas. I helped the moth fly away. Without that moth, I don't know how I would have pictured all that lay ahead of us. I was tired as a dog after that day at Mrs. J's and not just from washing the inside windows and watching Lee Ann. She was tired too, so we came on home, went to bed and slept all night.

Even hearing Mama and Walter begin to plan for Uncle David's boys to come while we were away at camp did not keep me awake. I knew that they would end up with those boys. I knew that Ms. Karney's talk about alcohol and abuse was just part of the process she uses for everybody, and that it was only a matter of time before those boys landed on us. Ms. Karney's whole job is to bounce kids around, and alcohol and abuse are her main ways of bouncing.

The real problem here is one she has no idea about: Keith Peller. He is a rapist waiting for the opportunity. This is how I came to see it with Angela's help. We came down a notch from serial killers. She has seen "Silence of the Lambs" too many times, she admits. But, I know enough about the world Ms. Karney operates in so I know that I cannot report suspicions about rape. I know that I can't tell Mama who would fly to the moon, and if I told Walter, he would simply shoot Keith Peller. Then we would have a murder trial on our hands. Mama and Lee Ann and I would be visiting the State Farm for the few weeks before Walter figured out how to hang himself in his cell. I know how everything would work out.

Picturing the way we will fly away to Aunt Helen in Texas like moths to Lee Ann is a lot easier, though it takes less talent than really going to Texas. I will have to pack double everything. Whatever Mama packs for camp, I will slip in twice that for the real trip to Texas. Two toothpastes, two towels, like Noah's Ark in a way.

July 25

...Ms. Karney came yesterday waving Lee Ann's teeth papers in one hand and the camp papers in the other. She looked like some kind of spider coming up the hill to the house, her arms going out in front, her legs coming on behind. Lee Ann has an appointment with the clinic tomorrow and the next day. She can have seven hundred and fifty dollars' worth of teeth put in her mouth in two days. Then on August first we go to camp. Ms. Karney drives us. She didn't look too happy that I was going to be along in the backseat, but Mama, who was feeling good for a change, went into the rose and its thorn, dog and his flea, planet and its moon, and finally got to Lee Ann and me on her list of two's that convinced Ms. Karney that I was going to Camp Independence, irregardless of rules, costs, policies, excuse my French.

July 26

...I don't like the plan any better than Ms. Karney does. Parts of it, I mean. I did like letting her spend her money for milkshakes—that's all she would buy us, because of Lee Ann's teeth situation. I could eat hamburgers just fine, I wanted to say, but since I was getting to save the money Mama gave us to buy something for lunch with, I zipped my lip and asked for two milkshakes, strawberry and chocolate. I almost puked, and hoped I would—all over her Toyota.

Lee Ann does look good with her new teeth in. Now I'll have to worry more about the Keith Pellers of the world who think they have the right to put their moves on any girl they please.

I planned how I would get us a seat up at the front of the bus and pretend that our parents were sending us to our Aunt Helen's house on Locust Avenue, Houston, Texas. Bus drivers, I bet, like that kind of story.

Ms. Karney acted okay, considering what she had to work with. Herself. She didn't try anything funny with papers or questions about our lives at home. Of course, we were in a clinic with about fifty dentists who are really students in dental school. She wanted to look important, so she filled in papers and sat by me as friendly as could be. I knew she hated me. It was mutual. But we sat and watched Lee Ann get done over. It took about two hours. It was a little like a beauty parlor. I have been to the dentist when one came in a trailer and parked at school. You know how I love a trailer, so I was happy to go in when my turn came. Some of the stupid Virginians cried. I had eleven caries, he called them. He couldn't understand why I still have baby teeth. I told him it was because I was adopted.

August 1

...Midnight...We are here at Camp Independence and unpacked. Lee Ann and I sneaked out to take our walk and made it all around the camp in the moonlight without anybody seeing us.

I don't think I'll have trouble getting us out of here. I saw a little sign for the Greyhound bus when we stopped for gas on the way here.

There are twenty cabins stuck on two sides of a little lake, up the hills from it. There are ramps to every door and the paths are like little highways, black and smooth, for the wheel chairs.

We got here about 4:30, and met our team leader, Pam, who is normal like me, I think. At least she looks okay. She is short and square-shaped with a pointy nose and big blue eyes. She laughs all the time and pulls at her hair that's twisted up in a crooked pony tail.

The camp motto is: I CAN DO IT. LET ME DO IT. We are supposed to yell this first thing every time we have a POW WOW. There are about a dozen small POW WOWs a day, Pam told us, and one big one every night after supper. We are divided up into Indian tribes. Lee Ann and I are Mohawks and have to think of a talent we have for the big final POW WOW, which I hope we won't be here for, because we will be on the road to Texas. But I'm going along with all the rules and regulations, except for not leaving the cabin after taps. They play a record, a very mournful one, over the loud speaker, and we have to learn the words to it by the end of camp. I guess I will have to learn faster if we want to know the words.

Then we had supper which I liked because it was what Mama calls city food—white bread, Kraft singles, canned plums and foamy milk, which I know is a sign of its being powdered milk. Maybe I should be a detective, the way I notice little things. They called it a picnic supper, but it wasn't like Mama's real picnics. It's a good thing I like anything from the city.

They don't have rules about smoking, which is another good thing and which surprised me. Of course, we had to listen about cancer and watch a movie about dying in a hospital. Lee Ann has to have her cigarette. Ms. Karney goes wild when she sees Lee Ann smoking. She says she looks like Edith Peeoff, but that it is very wrong for her to smoke. She brought us a record once of her singing, and we died laughing after she left. A dog would laugh if he heard those songs, or he'd howl his head off, which is what she sounded like the singer was doing.

It's a relief to be here after the ride with Ms. Karney, who kept a steady stream of advice to me about what to do for Lee Ann, what not to do, how to do it, how not to do it. Finally, I had to scream and jerk, pretending I saw a car coming out of a side road. I braced myself and squinted up my face like I thought we were about to wreck. That shut her up because she swerved and almost really did wreck the car. I should have known not to go that far, but she was bugging me to death. When she got to the Watch out for Boys, Don't let Them Bother your Sister, she isn't ready to handle Relationships or Sexual Advances, I thought I would puke again. I wished I'd had a couple of milkshakes to do a good job on her car. It's funny the way she takes herself so seriously. She forgets she's talking out of her head about caring about Lee Ann's being in the best home, but maybe she does think she knows best.

August 3

...It's lunch time at ole Camp Independence. The Mohawks have just had their third POW WOW and I volunteered to organize the talent show. I can do stuff like that with my eyes closed. I'll get it all ready so it can go on after we have left for Texas. I am sure the Mohawks will win. I know they would if Lee Ann and I could stay and do our pantomime-lip sync of some old Beatles' songs.

I'll have to rest up to write down what the handicaps are like here. It's a trip, as Angela's parents love to say. I have written to Angela but I will not mail it until we are out of here or almost.

I'll write down what the weirdest ones are like after I get some sleep. It's rest time now and I've got to sweet talk Pam into taking me into the gas station where the bus stops.

August 4

...The Pam idea stinks. She just looked at me like I was crazy when I asked her if she would mind running me over to the bus station. I didn't go into the Texas part or why, all the many reasons why, we were leaving Virginia. I just got as far as bus station in my speech.

"I am trained"—she did look like a hoot owl with her big pink glasses when she was talking, and her words did squeeze out of her face in hooey-hoos, too, just like the big old barn owl when he eats up mice and rats. "I love 'to spot' homesick campers. And one of the first, and I must tell you, best signs that a camper is about to split, is this old question about the bus station. Now you yourself have just asked that question, so what conclusion must I draw? I know because I am a former handicapped person who was a camper here."

I hate people who ask questions that they think have one answer. But forget that problem. You could have knocked me flat, I can tell you. I didn't know it was possible to get over being a handicap, so, naturally, I asked what she used to be. I had a few ideas of my own, based on the way her head wobbled a little and her left eye kept shutting. It was a chance out of the blue to ask her one of her own kind of questions.

Besides, it gave me some hope for Lee Ann. Maybe she could finish grade school, high school, and then, maybe, go on to a community college. She would be, maybe, thirty-seven when she finished.

I had my own answer for Pam, but I was pretending it was what my old fifth grade teacher called a DISCUSSION QUESTION. In other words, she could have her own opinions about her handicaps.

"I had so many," Pam said, proud as could be. "I don't know where to start."

"That's okay, I believe you," I said. Her answer fit perfectly with mine in my head, so I grabbed the conversation away from her and got back to my situation. I went on and on about how I was not a bit homesick, how I loved camp even though I was a normal person like she was now.

Didn't she know I was in charge of talent for the Mohawks for the last big POW WOW?

Her training with handicaps and camp had done one thing, for sure: it trained her not to believe a word she heard on earth. She did not believe me and had a sickening sweet, understanding look on her ugly face that I wanted to scrape off. She looked like a hoot owl, alright, except for her nose that looked like a baby's fist glued on.

If Jesus, himself, walked up to this Pam Roper and asked for a ride to the bus station so he could go save a bunch of communists or Catholics or just regular sinners, Pam would open up on him about her certification and training.

And, no sir, she would die before she'd give HIM a ride anywhere. I can hear her now. "You're just homesick, Jesus, so I want to give you some extra craft classes so when you do get to go home, you'll be taking some beautiful gifts for your loved ones."

Then she'd ask HIM some of her dumb, one-answer questions. I bet if she'd asked him the biggie, "Can a sinner like me be saved?" which is what the Jehovah Witnesses always say we should ask when they drop by to check on Mama, and I bet if Jesus really told the truth, he'd say "You've got a lot of work to do yet, young woman."

I don't think Jesus wants a bunch of sinners around him in heaven, ones who haven't done anything but act big. And while I'm on the subject, I don't really think Jesus would save someone as bad as Keith Peller even if he repented and begged and cried to be washed in the blood of the Lamb, not that Keith Peller would ever. I am sure that he doesn't think he did anything on earth to be sorry for, much less murder his friend. Keith Peller is the type person who doesn't think something is wrong if he doesn't get caught in the act. In fact, the real truth is that he doesn't think something is wrong, no matter what it is, if he is the one doing it.

If Uncle David wanted to lie down in the river and if he wanted to keep his head underwater, then, well, let him, so be it. If what he had just said to my Uncle David knocked him down, flat into the water, so to speak, and made him want to or need to lie down in the river, then, well, so be it, again.

If only I had been closer to the scene of the drowning instead of up the bluff on the blanket with Lee Ann last summer. Or if I could have been in the

134

boat, making it sink to the bottom in that shallow water, talking to Uncle David and not letting him get out of the boat to lie down by those rocks.

If I had seen Keith Peller hand over one of Lee Ann's pills, which is what I have been thinking may have happened, and if I had stuck out my arm and screamed something like, "Mama, Keith Peller stole Lee Ann's pill and is showing it to Uncle David, and now he is down at the river talking hateful to him." Well, what's the use of going on.

I'm afraid that I am turning into a person just like Mama, a "tame" hummingbird that won't leave a subject alone. I don't want to be that way. I want to be like boys are. They get up and leave things they can't change or die for. They do not think about things. Not the way girls do, anyway.

So I wasted a long time listening to Pam before I gave up on convincing her to do me this little bus-station-trip favor.

If she knew what was threatening my home—David Jr., Ernest and James Howard—she would see why I wanted to go to Texas, to test the waters there and see if Aunt Helen would be so happy she would move heaven and earth to keep us or move back to Virginia with us—do something to change the way things are. In fact, the very thought of being at home with things the way they are—Keith Peller sneaking up to the house from the woods, the boys either coming to live with us or not coming (either way will make Mama go around the bend)—makes me sick enough to buy me a ticket to the South Pole, forget Texas.

I thought I better not say exactly where it was I was going, and of course, Pam didn't have a whiff of my plan to take Lee Ann. She was so sure I wanted to run back home.

She wanted to talk about all her personal handicaps so I had to listen to soften her up. I learned from watching Jeannine in action with Uncle David that listening can turn a rock into a dandelion puff. It really can. That, I mean the listening, was the only difference I could see between Uncle David's two wives, I mean widows.

Mary Louise never listened to anybody. She did all the talking, and when it was something she had to know like what time her program did not come on because the President was announcing something big, then she couldn't stand it because she had to hear some facts with her ears from somebody besides herself.

But anyway, Pam was running off at the mouth about her thirty percent hearing loss, her retina that had to be stitched up—yeah, I could see the doctor hadn't had his needle threaded—her Perth's disease that kept her in a wheelchair for two years, and I forget what all. "It's amazing," I said, "to look at you now." I was lying because she looked like Big Bird—Lee Ann loves him, but I don't—in a tight pair of khaki pants with ten pockets which I counted as she was talking about her challenges.

But it all boiled down to NO. Pam was not going to take me anywhere "off the premises" because now she was a Camp Counselor and had been trained in spotting homesick symptoms, and then she announced

136

the cure—Crafts. I had to go through a speeded-up, double schedule of camp events so I couldn't think. Just try to keep an honor roller from thinking. Try it. But I had to go along with her cure and pretend that it was all making me happier.

But now it's night and I can write in my book with the flashlight under my chin. My neck is stiff from holding it so long, but who cares?

I must admit that without the help of the ex-handicap Pam Roper, I don't see how I can get us to Texas. I wouldn't be a bit surprised if Ms. Karney didn't stick her Dracula face into this deal and put Pam up to keeping a bird's eye view on Lee Ann and me. I can't prove it, but that's what I'll think until I'm DEAD AND GONE. If you have to prove everything you know, you will be DEAD AND GONE before you could gather up all the facts.

Those beautiful words make me sleepy, so I'll quit, but I think I'll have to go along with this camp thing until I figure out something else. Here I am, almost out of Virginia, as far as Danville almost, but hung up by an ex-handicap.

August 10

...The cure for homesickness is having a terrible side effect: curing me of my dream of getting Lee Ann and me to where we belong—Texas. Maybe if I write some about Uncle David's hellions, Davey Jr., Ernest and James Howard, it will spark up my dream and get me going.

Pam put me in charge of the salad bowl class and the popsicle stick crafts, plus I had double swimming (I couldn't get out of taking life-saving, and I don't mind it as much as I thought I would) and nature walks, not to mention the talent contest practices, so I have not figured out a new way to get us out of here. I did enjoy myself a little, I admit, acting know-it-all, but-sweet-about-it, like a teacher. Even if my students were weird beyond weird. Reruns of Twilight Zones. When they finished their little stick sailboats, they were thrilled with their sad, poor selves. They were every bit as happy as I will be when I get us to Texas. I'll just write a few sentences about the worst boys on earth to remind me of why we have to get away to Texas for a little while anyway. I wish we could just go back home for a visit. Maybe for a funeral, someone close, not Mama or Walter, of course, and not one of the boys. Someone like Angela's Gram who is so old and sick that there is no other way to go, but she is already almost Dead and Gone.

Let me put it this way: Uncle David's boys will grow up, I bet, into Keith Pellers if they don't come to live with us, and they may grow up to be Keith Pellers even if they do come live with us. Even James Howard, and he still looks innocent. "Looks" is the operative word in that sentence.

"Going on nineteen," Mama says.

I'll start with James Howard. He should have been named James Earl Ray, she says. We all expect the worst. Lee Harvey would suit him better as a name I think.

James Howard has a thing for emergency rooms and rescue squads. He has been in hospitals so much that he is known all over. They call him "The Kid." He goes on a regular basis to the one in Lynchburg and he's been to all of them in Richmond. He'll cut himself just to get to ride in a rescue wagon, with the siren going. I don't really think he minded his own daddy drowning because of all the rescue stuff going on. If he could talk, which he can't and maybe won't (because if we are right about it, he is funny in the head), he'd call up the rescue wagon on the phone.

If he could talk, he could tell us what happened down at the river because he was found later sitting on a rock just off the path down to the river, out of the way, so no one knew he was there, like a frog in the shade, just sucking his thumb and twisting his hair at the same time. That's his only talent, so far, unless you count surviving his mother, stepmother and foster mother.

I think the reruns of "The Fall Guy" got him off to a bad start. Mary Louise used to prop him up in front of a table TV with a bottle holder and leave him for hours. She said most babies didn't have television.

Anyway, that's James Howard who may live to see first grade. I don't think he talks yet, not English anyway. He just has fits when he doesn't like what's going on. That's why they can't find any more foster parents and why he's back in the group home or orphanage. Jeannine is doing her part, she told Mama, to keep the boys together—not together in the usual sense of being in one house. So when James Howard gets thrown back in the orphanage, she snatches Davey Jr. and Ernest back from their foster homes too. She does this over the phone. She has some kind of long distance custody that is more powerful than Mary Louise's being their blood mother. No one understands it, and Mama thinks she does it to lend credibility to herself as a beneficiary and heir to Uncle David's house and life insurance.

Ernest is the oldest one, the quietest, but Mama says it's the quiet ones that you have to watch. That's why she says she never worries about me. I'm a talker. She says she'll never go crazy because she can communicate her troubles and then they don't seem so big. She says I'm safe in the same way from mental disease. I don't know if she's right or not.

Ernest is mean, I know this for a fact. He used to stick nails in the old horse in Mr. Simms' field. He'd get him to come over to the fence with an apple, and then he'd jump on his back. The horse didn't mind at all and that's what I would have liked, just to sit on a big red horse by the fence in the shade and pretend to gallop after Indians. No way, for Ernest. He got on the old horse and then stuck in the nail and they flew off. Ernest would have ridden him to death, I believe, but the horse outsmarted him, which didn't take much, and ran straight into the tree. It might have hurt the horse some, but it also threw Ernest against the tree and worked him over "good" as Walter said, and damaged him but not the tree too much, which is what the horse must have been thinking.

Davey Jr. is the next one, and he's hung up on money. So much that he steals what he can't make from doing jobs. He'll do anything for money and nothing unless you pay him. He tried once to stop eating and let us pay him to start up again.

Uncle David said why not, but Mama hit the fan when she heard about it and straightened that little money-making scheme out.

Writing about my cousins, and I thank Jesus we're not blood cousins, makes me all the more dead set on not going back home until we have gone to Texas. Who knows, maybe Aunt Helen will beg us to live with her.

Texas or Bust. I think I'd rather be a hostage in one of the foreign countries than go home right now. Yes, I would.

August 11

...I have made a big discovery! About how to get along with people: Throw Fits. I'm so used to bossing Lee Ann, who doesn't count because she is not a normal person, or being bossed by any grownup that I never knew that I could stretch myself and boss grown, normal people back.

But if I throw a fit to get their attention, I can almost make them forget that I am young. I have to be charged up to really work myself up into a raging coniption fit. Grownups learn to condense fits down into a smile that's as thin as this ball point line of ink, _____ or to a look as hot as fire, or a shrug cold as a rock in December. I have seen all these condensed fits at one time or another.

Mama has her fits in talking and I have recorded how they go on and on in this book. I wish she could put a lid on hers a little, but then she wouldn't be Mama, I guess. She doesn't think people can change, except get worse. I think that's what keeps her from changing herself.

Until I got here to Camp Independence, I didn't have time to just sit around and figure out why what had already happened, happened. Or how people throw their fits, or what shapes the fits take. But with all this empty time, a bunk bed to lie on and a Zero bar to eat because they were out of Baby Ruth's, I can think away like crazy.

Now, I have everything straight about the past. For the time being, anyway. I could put it all in two or three sentences, but I'm so worried about the future which I can't put down in two or three sentences or even two or three notebooks, because it's so mixed up with what might happen if I...or if I...or if Mama...or if...or if the boys...or if Keith Peller...or if Aunt Helen... The only if that is a happy one is the one that says if Keith Peller dies or moves to Nebraska.

Now I know the value of a vacation or why those old monks liked to live in stone monasteries shut off from the rest of the world. I have studied World History under Mrs. Dot Vaughn and my favorite part was the Dark Ages. That was a beautiful time in the history of the world. Everybody had a job he was born into, like making barrels or wagon wheels, weaving dresses, making shoes, building castles and cathedrals. No, they did not have to go and find work like Walter and Mama, who are always looking for houses to rebuild or paint or to put in the electricity or chickens to debeak or old women to wash and feed. Or Uncle David getting into the job of painting in Lynchburg, which I call Lunchbox and now hate on principle, a job which led to him meeting Keith Peller and Jeannine, not to mention her hateful Linda Jo. And that led to the wedding where Mama hollered and cried and tried to pass it off as happiness. And that led to Uncle David's drowning. Now it's clear how one little thing led to the big thing in our lives. And the drowning led to the problem of THE BOYS coming to live with us

143

which led the Ick-face Ms. Karney to our house, and Keith Peller to think he could come into our bedroom and do something to Lee Ann and now we are having to go—of course we also want to go—to Texas. Not to mention Ms. Karney's investigation of how we take care of Lee Ann much less three pre-criminals, (the boys) and now is leading to me becoming The Run Away Kid with my sister so we can get away from all these things leading to something we don't want: the something terrible I feel coming.

So, if we were living back in the Dark Ages, none of all that has happened to us would have happened. Walter would have been sure of his job (not in Texas, of course, and not as a pumper on an oil rig, of course). Chickens would scratch around the back doors of the castles with their own beaks still on their heads and all the old ladies would be dead and buried from the plague or childbirth. There were plenty of orphans, so I would be there, and Lee Ann.

In the beautiful Dark Ages, some people did nothing but pray, but they had to, what with a plague coming at regular intervals, not like now, when AIDS does not sweep through a city plague-style, but sneaks up on people who don't know how to be mature and responsible about intercourse or drugs and just get carried away thinking only of how they feel at that moment. We would wear maroon velvet cones on our heads with little wispy veils hanging from the peaks and we would lean out of narrow windows waving at friends riding over the meadows to visit us or shoot our enemies with arrows from high, slanted slits in the stone walls. Then we would watch them die slowly on the plains in front of our castle.

I learned about AIDS prevention when we were studying how not to get pregnant. I mean the teacher didn't call it that because a lot of people are against sex education in the seventh grade, but that is what it was, and since we never got Lee Ann her no-baby operation, I listened twice as hard—once for her and once for me, for when I am grown and have to deal with the hassles of having babies and boyfriends and husbands (the worst). It was clear to me then that Keith Peller was thinking that he could have himself a little free sex, a little fun with Lee Ann—I know how his mind works—because she can't tell anyone what happened. He probably has considered killing me, but that would be the day. He is too much of a coward to kill someone outright—put his hands around a throat, pull a trigger. He goes for the arranged accident, like maybe the day at the river. But because I am aware of that part of his slime-nature, I know that I can take care of myself and Lee Ann. She will never be alone with him so he cannot rape her. No one was ever raped with a sister watching, I mean, a regular rape. I know there are war situations and gang rapes, but I never have heard of a civilian rape with a sister (me) there screaming and stabbing kitchen knives in the rapist's back. I have it all figured out—that part. I am not afraid of being killed by Keith Peller, but I am afraid of his ruining our lives as we live them. So, going to Texas will definitely change the way we are living our lives and all for the good as I see it.

145

In the Dark Ages, many, many people died of the plague or went to a monastery. That sentence would make a nice opening to a history test question.

Lee Ann would have been one of the dead ones or maybe we could have sat on a street corner and begged. Then she would have thrashed herself to death if the plague hadn't got her first. I think afflicted people were made into clowns and went to castles with circuses, which would not be at all bad when you think about it.

But it's hard to say what would have been the situation of someone like Lee Ann back then. I shouldn't count on her absolute safety back then knowing as little as I do.

Once you know her ways, you can get her to do anything you please. That's why, to go back a little, I had to push her down the stairs at home when Keith Peller was sweet talking and preparing the way for sex. I wonder if he has sneaked back and seen that we are gone. That will stump him.

You have to get to understand how Lee Ann is tied to the pill schedule and does funny stuff if you change it even by a few minutes. Thrashing is the hardest to deal with, I guess, but her long sleeps aren't so hot either. Trying to wake her up when she's had two pills too close together is like trying to talk to a dead person. She could be put in the trunk of a car and kidnapped and never even realize it until it was too late. If the kidnappers weren't real criminals, it wouldn't be too bad of an experience.

August 12

...I see how many ideas I write down when I'm at Camp on vacation. Even on my double duty schedule that Pam thinks will get rid of my homesickness, I have plenty of time to think and write, compared to at home where things are jumping at me all the time. People say to me here, the counselors from the city, "How quiet it must be in the country. So peaceful." I want to say back, "Yeah, do you have a drowned uncle and three wildcats coming to live with you and an epileptic sister who has her social worker who may try to take her away from her parents and sister?"

I still think that running away forever was a good thought, but I will settle for vacation with Aunt Helen in Texas. I'll give Lee Ann two pills and put her in the trunk of the car that's taking us to Texas, but whose car is that, Miss Crystal Ball?

I don't know. Yet. I'll have to lie here and think some more, so goodbye 'til I die, tell a lie. That's how Angela and I always hang up on each other.

August 13

...I got us a car with a trunk and of all things, it's a state police car! Trooper Harris comes every day to time the wheelchair races with his portable radar machine, and his big blue and black car has a huge trunk that does not have a thing in it but that little radar thing. That is the only car I can spot that will hold the both of us. Everyone else drives a van or a 4 X 4 and you can't hide a cup of water in a van from the driver.

Trooper Harris stays until dark and helps with the POW WOWs. One of the retards here is his kid Tracy, so he's real nice to everyone. I've seen him leave his trunk open, and I believe I can get Lee Ann to walk over to it and get in. I'll take pillows and she'll be asleep in no time.

How I'm going to convince him not to bring us right straight back here or back home or to jail is a challenge. I admit it. Throwing a fit, a sad one with a sick grandma in it is what I have in mind. She, my poor Grannie, lives in Danville near the bus station. Get it? Somehow, I'll get us that far and have to work on it from there. It is a very good thing that I am as smart as I am. Anybody not as smart as I am would give up on getting to Texas.

So much was happening at one time, I don't know if I can put it all down in sentences on paper.

Here is how I kidnapped ourselves away from Camp Independence. It was almost dark, about nine o'clock. Trooper Harris was giving the Wheelies, that's what they call themselves, an extra practice for the final relays on Friday. He was concentrating on his pitiful Wheelie daughter Tracy. She didn't have a prayer of winning, but he kept starting the races over to let her have a better (head) start. I could see a soft spot in him for Tracy who was terrible to look at even if you were her blood kin. Her hair grew in tufts like tails all over her head and I don't know why she couldn't walk. Noticing that soft spot for Terrible Tracy and for all the Wheelies, I saw Trooper Harris as our way out of Virginia. You can't beat pity for making things easier.

In the parking lot after supper, the Wheelies were racing on the asphalt that felt like black velvet. They could do amazing things in their wheelchairs. I wish Lee Ann and I had two of the electric ones, but we couldn't use them at home. No sidewalks, but we sure could race in Texas.

I folded Lee Ann up like a pocket knife by grabbing her around the waist from behind and bending her over frontwards. I'm stronger than I look. Then I leaned her up against the edge of Trooper Harris' car trunk which was open just as I planned for it to be. Then I toppled her down in it onto the two pillows and blankets, I had dropped in like it was a mistake of some kind.

Trooper Harris was making like Rambo to all the kids. So he didn't even look at us over by his car. I got

150

us scrunched back in the dark and crumpled up the black trash bag—I took it from the kitchen—all over us.

We looked like black air, I mean we looked like nothing was there in his trunk. Nothing that wasn't supposed to be. I had packed a little bag of Lee Ann's pills, some Zero bars, a hairbrush and some clean shorts and tee-shirts. It wasn't time for either one of us to get the curse, as Mama calls it, so I didn't need extras, just a toothbrush, and one for the both of us.

So at that point the plan is going fine: Lee Ann is dead asleep, straightened out like a stick of gum. I am next to her like another stick of gum. In a little bit, Trooper Harris tosses in his three-legged radar machine and slams the trunk. I'm expecting it so I push us back out of the way.

Then, for the first time in my life, I felt what Mama says she feels every day—overwhelmed. Big time. Locked in the trunk with an epileptic sister. Trying to get to Texas from a camp in the mountains of Virginia. I felt pretty much like crying, but decided to eat a Zero instead.

The hundred dollar bills helped me feel way better and they were flattened out in the bottom of my Puma tennis shoes, but I could feel them there and they made me feel like I was walking on money, which of course, I was, even though I was stretched out with my sister in the trunk of a police car.

I took some comfort in the fact that locked up in the trunk of a state trooper's car, for God's sake, we were safe as a person can be on earth. I guess. No Keith Pellers could get inside a state trooper's trunk. No Siree Bob. That's what Mama says a lot. At least

151

there were no Ms. Karneys getting Lee Ann to put her mark on a paper telling how she had been a victim of abuse.

I began to think of that trunk as if it were my own little Dark Ages. It didn't have modern conveniences, and it was very, very dark, but don't worry, I had made us, the both of us, go to the bathroom just before I loaded us in, so to speak.

So, after I got to thinking along those Dark Ages lines, I saw that riding along in the cool August night in a state police car was not a bad way to spend time. I thought when he'd have to get his radar machine out the trunk, then I'd have to come up with some excuse for why we were laid up in his car like two matches in a box, only not as straight.

The match thing got me to thinking some more. And when I start thinking, can't anything or anybody stop me. I would throw a fit. Like a match, I'd just strike up into a little fire. I know grown people think kids are normal and can do right, so it scares them shitless, as Keith Peller used to say when he was around and was talking, when a kid goes nuts.

Sure enough, when we got to where we were going and which turned out to be, thank God—Danville, Trooper Harris did open up his trunk and get his radar thing out. I rattled the black plastic we were under. He must have thought it was a snake or a chipmunk or something because he said, "Damn, something's wild in here!"

He poked at us with a stick. I was afraid it was a gun, but he didn't shoot us.

Time for my fit: I let loose and tore up that plastic and leaped out of that car trunk.

Let me explain that by then it was pitch dark and just his red parking lights were on, so it looked like some kind of ninety-seven-pound wild animal sure enough was flying out of his trunk.

God was helping me because at that very time, Lee Ann went into her best thrashing style.

Moaning and groaning and yipping like a coyote or wolf and rolling all around in the trunk, getting all wrapped up in the black plastic. It was grand. But, I still had no idea about what to say in my fit when it came time to put it into words. Blubbering and heaving can go on only so long before they'll take you to an emergency room and give you a shot to shut you up. So I was trying to think, as well as keep all the commotion going strong, but it was so much noise and thrashing and flapping plastic and the Trooper yelling down at the legs and arms flailing and flinging. "Whut th' Hell, Whut th' Hell?"

That's what he kept on yelling down into the trunk even though I had thrown myself out of the trunk and was grinding around in the dirt near his feet, first on my stomach, then on my butt. Things went on like that for about eight minutes, I guess. Then the big dummy thought to get out his two-foot flashlight and shine it on us. I wished Lee Ann had not got her new teeth in, because her thrashing, toothless face would have been something else. It would have stopped an army of state police.

Even with her teeth, it was not a pretty sight. I let my hair down and it was matted up in the dirt and

153

swinging around in little hot burning whisks when it hit him in the face, which it did as many times as I could manage by jumping up and tossing all of my hair over my head and then jerking it down real fast.

I would make a very good freedom fighter and wouldn't need guns. In fact, I think I could train the guerillas. But back to my troubles at the time.

I learned in the school this year how to get out of answering a teacher's question. Just ask one back in the place of hers. Well, I applied that little piece of knowledge to my situation, as agitated as I was and even though I had to keep one eye rolling like crazy (which I have practiced and practiced when there wasn't anything much to do, and living in Virginia, I could practice many times) on Lee Ann so she didn't get too cut up or banged up in the trunk. At home, we make sure she has her plenty of room to thrash in.

Okay. How did I use what I learned in school? I asked back to Trooper Harris, "What Th' Hell do you think you're doing driving off from Camp Independence with us locked up in the trunk?" Add in a lot of blubbers and heaves and you'll have what I asked him.

It took him some time to splutter that he did not drive off from Camp, etc. etc. etc.

I took up some extra time by saying, "Well, who da Hell took us away if you didn't?" Blubber, etc.

He tried to answer the stupid question with a stupider answer like, "Yes, I mean I was the driver, but how was I to know you were in my trunk?"

Etc., etc.

This trash went on until I said we better get my sister who was epileptic out of his trunk and give her some medicine. I let him watch her thrash a little bit more to scare him while I went on with my blubber and dry heaves act. I love a chance to cuss.

He was jelly by the time we started pulling Lee Ann out of the trunk. She goes stiff after thrashing and then she goes limp. The stiffness lasts about three minutes and if you have never been around a person like Lee Ann, it could make you think you have a dead person on hand.

And of course, I was counting on just that fact. Trooper Harris' hair almost turned white in front of my eyes. I felt a little sorry for him.

He changed from saying, "Whut th' Hell" to "O my God." I let him go on for a while with that. Then as Lee Ann started going limp, I said we better take her into his house, which was a nice little apartment with not a tree or blade of grass in sight. Pure city.

"Is this Danville?" I asked him, calm as anything and cutting off my fit like a light switch.

He was in no shape to notice my fit had passed, that I was brushing myself off and pulling my hair back into a ponytail holder. I keep extras on my wrists and have started a new fashion in my Talented and Gifted Program by wearing these as bracelets. I could feel the money in my shoes, and I felt fresh as a daisy although I could see by his watch it was 12:30.

"It's Danville, alright."

So then I knew we had made the first part of our trip to Texas. I felt proud, though I didn't have a clue about what he was going to do with us when he got us

155

in his apartment. I knew it was too late and too far to drive us back to Camp, and I knew he was not going to get back in the car with Lee Ann. I felt very strong and powerful, like a freedom fighter should, to have a State Police asking me what we should do.

"She needs a flat bed or sofa to lie out or down on. She needs a piece of bread to eat with her pill. She hasn't had a mouthful but a Zero, since we were locked up in your trunk, by mistake, and that was three hours ago."

"Yeah, you can tell me about it when we get her straight." He did have some sympathy for Lee Ann, but she didn't need all that he was pouring on her. It was gooey, the way he kept sighing and talking to himself about Tracy and the kids at Camp and how Tracy's mother, I guess she was the bitch he kept mentioning, had run off. I started to tell him my own story, about how I was really from Texas, how my real mother had to go to Salt Lake City to pursue her dream, but he wasn't calm enough to take it in. Anyway, you have to dole out the truth to grownups in medicine dropper amounts. They can't take it except that way.

We got Lee Ann into his nice apartment, neat as Uncle David's tool box. We stretched her out on one of his twin beds and he went and got her a piece of bread. "It's rye," he said.

"We know rye. It will do." I was being kind and careful of his feelings.

"Now," he says as he opens up a Bud, "how come you two got yourselves locked up inside of my trunk, and let me drive three hours from Camp to Danville, without hollering and banging to get me to stop?"

He was getting worked up again by saying, "This is all I need." He said it two, maybe three times, and I didn't interrupt to let him get it out of his system.

"To tell the truth," which there was no way I could, and had no idea what was going to fall out of my mouth, except for one thing: it would not be the truth, "We thought it was some kind of game at Camp to be locked up in the police car to be driven around a little. Then I fell asleep, and Lee Ann, she had taken her nighttime medication, (I say medication instead of pills when I talk to some people), so, we honestly did not know where we were being driven to."

Can you believe it, whoever is reading my book? He went for it hook, line and sinker. I guess he didn't have much choice, and I know from practicing in front of the mirror at home how I look when I'm telling lies. Like a little angel, except I'm skinny and have long straight brown hair and all the pictures I have seen of angels are fat and have curly yellow hair. It must be left over from when I was a baby–my angel look. I understand that I was a fat baby and had curls that were so blonde they were white.

Then because he was so upset, though he looked a lot better than he had for thirty minutes, he asked me what we should do.

"Let my sister–she's not my real one, she and I are both adopted–get her rest. If she doesn't get it, you can't tell which way she might jump." I stopped looking like the angel and started looking my important, serious look. He paid close attention to me as if I was the teacher, and he had just failed the make-up test.

157

"We came to Camp Independence from Houston, Texas. Our address is 713 Locust. Our zip code is 76706."

Wasn't I smart to slip in the zip instead of the phone number? Being so detailed about one thing threw him off track about the other details. And to think he's in Law Enforcement. If he's a State Trooper, I could be head of the F.B.I.

"We need to go back to Houston early from Camp because our Aunt Helen, the adopted one, is sick. As a dog," I added, "with CANCER of the throat. She can hardly talk. She's still at home because they haven't made her go to the hospital yet, but I'm afraid if we don't hurry back on the Greyhound we may MISS seeing her."

Again, God was busy helping me out. Seems Trooper Harris had a dead grandma, from CANCER. And she did not get to die at home, but if he had to do it all over again she would. I think Tracy and her mom were mixed up in all the sadness he was feeling. Also, he was on some kind of probation and did not need us locked in his trunk. How would this look on his record, he asked the ceiling.

The upshot of it all was that the next day after a delicious breakfast at the Waffle House, we bought our ticket and are riding high for Texas, as I write this story down for others to read when we are DEAD AND GONE which won't be for a very long time, if my luck keeps working the way it has recently.

By the time Mama and Walter get the news of our departure (Isn't it funny how in my mind, our running away has become an important sounding word like

"Departure," I guess It's from riding Greyhound and hearing so many announcements. "DEPARTING GATE 13, BUS NUMBER 37, DEPARTURES FOR ALL POINTS SOUTH AND WEST." It's beautiful, I think.), I'll have us good and settled with Aunt Helen. If things don't work out—if Mama threatens to have a heart attack, we'll come back.

I told Trooper Harris we had enough, but he kicked in a hundred. That's what we'll come back on, IF we have to. I'm counting on Mama's love of pen pals to let us stay on in Texas. She would certainly have a steady stream of letters. I'm also counting on her being driven crazy by Uncle David's boys if they do come.

They ought to get Ms. Karney straight. If she looks at them, they'll set her Toyota on fire. She will soon learn to appreciate the fact that those boys are at the end of the line foster-parents-wise. No one else on earth would have them, so she had better stop investigating them.

Walter might be mad enough to jump in his truck and drive down here and pick us up when he realizes what I have done. But he'd enjoy the trip and we could eat sardine and onion sandwiches on the way back to Virginia to make him happy.

I know it'll all work out, and if it does not, this book will explain why and how what happened. I'm changing the name of my book from the beautiful and sad DEAD AND GONE to LOCAL SPEED, which are the words on a road sign, one I saw a few towns back, because those words describe the way I have to live my life and the way I have to live Lee Ann's life for her too. And it's Angela's way of talking about drugs, which I

159

think is cool and certainly applies to me handing out pills to Lee Ann. She can read that sign, in her way which means I whisper the words to her and she nods. Local Speed, Angela has told me, was available at the high school when we were discussing drugs. I will think of Lee Ann's pills as LOCAL SPEED and feel powerful, and I will think of my book by that name and feel smart.

She is having a wonderful time so far on the trip. I have her prescription and am sure I can refill it at one of the little drug stores on the way. The new title is happier, too. Like me.

I couldn't get us on the express line to Texas that goes interstate and has you there in two days. I had to get us on the local that will take about two and a half days. One day to stay in Texas, and then, bingo, back on the Greyhound and heading back home. Unless Aunt Helen cannot bear for us to leave. On this bus, we stop everywhere. People are very nice to us just like I expected. Ms. Karney and Keith Peller are the only two people I've met who did not treat Lee Ann right, and they were at home. I will stop writing now, feeling great because I am doing what needed to be done and also what I wanted to do—figure out things, leave Virginia and head for Texas. When I want to become a movie star or doctor, I'll take it, as the good alcoholics say, the ones to go for treatment, one step at a time.

160

August 14

...I am having second thoughts. I hate second thoughts. They usually drain off all the fun from a thing. In this case, too.

I am, I am sorry to say, having second thoughts about going to Texas, even though here we are just pulling out of Greensboro, North Carolina, after a very nice, expensive lunch of chili dogs and cheesecake in little plastic containers the exact size of the dog and cake. We're riding on to Charlotte, that's the next stop, but I'm second thinking. What we should do when we get to Charlotte has got me going, as Walter would say. I guess he would have a lot to say about our situation. He would ask me how in God's name was I going to get Lee Ann from the bus station in Houston to, well, where the hell? He would say that. It's one thing to go from city to city, little local nowheres like Eden, North Carolina, to Thomasville, and it is another damn sight to go to a city to live where you don't know the first person. He would say that, throwing in a few more cuss words. He would think I hadn't thought of those things. Then because he is a man and can't help thinking about sex, he would begin to worry about Lee Ann and strange men and her getting pregnant. To him, getting pregnant is as bad as getting AIDS. He never worries about me getting either one. He's right about both because I am mature and responsible.

And being mature and responsible makes me have these second thoughts. We should turn around and go on back home. It has been so pleasant to be out of Virginia, to ride way over the local speed limits. I get us seats behind the driver and keep my eye on the speed. This one is hitting eighty. My new friend Trooper Harris should see this bus boogying on down the road. But I better get serious and at least think about cashing in our tickets and turning around.

It will be exciting. I figure we'll get home just about the time we were supposed to be coming back from Camp Independence. Everybody will be mad as hell at us--me, I mean. They will just have gotten serious about looking for us.

Trooper Harris is probably fired by now. Maybe he ought to be, for being so dumb. We caught him off guard and took advantage of him. But why shouldn't we?

What got me going is the way Lee Ann's been acting the last hour. We're both thrown off from understanding each other by this traveling. And I can't let her thrash here on the bus, so I step up the pills to keep her quiet. Because the bus stops a lot and different people are getting on and off, no one thinks it's strange that she sleeps most of the time. And we've only been on our trip to Texas two days, not counting the night with Trooper Harris, which does not really count as traveling. Riding in a trunk is not traveling. Greyhound is.

But my point is that Lee Ann is trying to get something across to me. I think part of the trouble is, I do not want to hear what she is telling me, what I think

162

she is telling me. Also, she is crying a little. Not much. Also, she is looking scared.

There's no reason to. We are in America. I have one hundred and eighty-seven dollars left in my shoes.

FOUR

August 15

...To Houston was 98.73, each, one way, so I have some change left, and one hundred and eighty-five dollars in bills. Two dollars in my pocket, the rest in my backpack. I'll have just enough to get us home if that's what we do, and we can live on candy bars. I am over my little sinking spell, as Mama calls it, about turning around and going home.

When any woman gets on the bus, but especially one about Mama's age and size, that's when I see trouble. Lee Ann leans toward her, and tries to go sit by her. All I have to do is pull a little on Lee Ann's arm and she sits back in her seat, but I can tell she is missing Mama.

She's not by herself. I got one woman on a talking jag and it made me right homesick again wanting to hear Mama work herself up on our favorite subjects—Uncle David's drowning, the two people who killed him even though it looked like a drowning-under-the-influence, how Mary Louise, bad as she was, was just a warm-up for Jeannine Turner and Keith Peller who waltzed themselves into our lives, caused the death of a good man, stole his home, sold it for cash, and put his kids in foster homes so Mama felt she would have to make every effort to get the boys to come live with her when she herself already has two adopted daughters, one afflicted.

I miss Angela so much my rib cage aches. I say rib cage instead of heart because I do not want to make it hurt worse. I miss my real mother too, but not as much as I miss Mama and Angela. I have her letters from Utah with me which is all I have ever had so it's not as if I had not had time to get used to missing her.

Maybe my trip to Texas and being with Aunt Helen again just for a little while—well, okay, so far it's only to North Carolina, but it is still a trip toward Texas, will be Mama's subject after she hears about it.

Maybe our running away will help her ease up on Uncle David's death. When and if I tell her the whole truth about Keith Peller and what he had in mind and what Lee Ann's fall down the steps really meant, the whole thing, I feel sure Mama will have something refreshing to talk about. I mean it will be a change for her. And with my cousins—not blood ones—maybe there at home by now—I bet my life that they are there—Mama will have problems that will take her mind off last summer.

Another woman just got on at Concordia. Lee Ann will wake up and want to go sit by her. I wouldn't mind myself. She looks as complicated and good and dangerous as my own Mama—not the blood one in Utah, but my own Mama in Virginia.

When I think about it, my real mother was and maybe still is those three things. Maybe all mothers are. The bus is now picking up and passing by twenty, the local speed of fifty-five.

167

August 16

...I'm surprised to see that we are in a place I didn't plan at all for us to be in. A house in Salisbury, North Carolina. And what a house this one is. As Miss Linda Jo Turner would say, an OOH LA LA house: swimming pool with a little house that looks like a cave in a rock, only the rock is so light I can pick it up, I mean I can pick up the cave and all. That's where you change into your bathing suit. And inside the real house there are little short fountains with statues of frogs and naked girls. There's a running creek in the living room with gold fish in it and trees in pots bunched up in the curves of the creek. Over in the corner is a big rock fireplace with an electric fire so they can have winter, they say, when they want it, and summer by the little creek. I know I have to explain who this "they" are, and I will slowly because I am tireder than I have ever been in my life.

Sometimes they have winter and summer at once and said we could have a cookout there tonight. I told them I'd promised Lee Ann some tacos so they changed and said they'd take us to a Tex-Mex place.

In such a nice spot, I could not worry about things for a while because at least we were heading for Texas in a way.

We're stopped, you could say we are trapped here in Salisbury, N.C., with two nut-case ladies who laugh a lot real loud and then get serious instantly. They call us Juju Fruits and fix us snacks all the time.

Right now, I can hear them fighting over what they should do with us, but because I have now been awake for more than twenty-three hours, I am not following it as well as I should.

The one named Bess is some kind of foreigner with kin people in New Jersey and Florida. She has an American accent and wears sweats and Nikes so it's hard to tell where she comes from originally. The other one is Pat. They have lived in Utah. They like us, at least, they say they do, and believed me right off about taking Lee Ann to Texas to visit our Aunt Helen. I left out the cancer part. People always fall for aunts who would not hurt a fly. Who has ever heard of a mean aunt? I know there are some out there, but not many.

I think they are fighting right now upstairs over whether to drive us to Texas or take us back to Virginia. I mentioned Utah as a possibility, and that turned them onto their Utah stories. Of course, they think their little stories have turned me against Utah, but that will never happen.

Still, I don't think I can talk them into driving us to Utah. Maybe next summer.

They hate Utah from having lived there a couple of years while they studied computers.

These "girls"—they call themselves girls, but are deep into their fourth decade as Mama would say—are rich and work here in their basement which is lined around the wall with every kind of computer. They let Lee Ann and me play games all morning when we got here from the bus station and restaurant. I took Sis's turns for her. Mist and Doom are pretty neat, even if I got tired of them after a few hours, but could not go to sleep because of being in a new place, and I said that we would not be needing a bed, but would just rest a short while.

What happened was this: they saw the policeman talking to us at the bus station and me crying—I can make tears come down all over my tee shirt just by thinking of some of the sad things I know—like Uncle David in the river and being dragged up the bank—Bess and Pat came over and told him there had been some mistake and that they were meeting us and would take us home. I went along with it because at that point, I was near the end of my rope. I was losing my grip on the situation. I hate to say it, but I was.

I didn't know then, and don't care now, what those two women were doing in a bus station at two in the morning, but I thought they would be better to deal with than the policeman. Runaway girls are always automatically thought of as child prostitutes, no matter how young, no matter how epileptic. I wasn't born yesterday, as Mama says, and I knew I was too tired to deal with being thought of as a prostitute. If we looked like prostitutes, then I pity to see what the paying customers would look like, but I know selling sex does not depend on looks, and I know rape victims can be old ladies or epileptics especially if the rapist is Keith Peller or like him, and I guess all rapists are.

I didn't think it would be smart to ask either of the women, who turned out to be Bess and Pat, in front of the policeman, what in the world they were doing in the bus station, or say I had never seen them (or anything close to them) in my life, and later I didn't think it would be polite to ask them or worth listening to their answers in my condition which was almost terminal, going, going, gone, as I said. I felt like a soldier must feel on a battle field, wounded, needing water and a transfusion, any kind of help, big-time.

And there was the new problem of Lemuel Foster Craigwall. He was a kid, not much bigger than me, who came over to us in the bus station—not even a backpack on him. He looked as bad as we felt. Could we help him? No, we could not, but he went on anyway as if we were grown up middle aged, middle class people who were looking for ways to improve the world instead of two girls trying to survive the mess, I admit, I got us into.

A formal introduction followed as if he were going to ask us to a prom "I am Lemuel Foster Craigwall," he begins. "And I am Amelia Earhart," I wanted to say, he was so ridiculous, so white-bread as we say at school, so prep, but I managed a cool, "So?"

It turns out that he had been left by his friends when he asked them to stop to let him get a drink. When he runs in to get change for the machine, thinking that they will fill up with gas since they have stopped to let him get his Arizona tea with raspberry, he was going to get everyone in the car a drink, they drive off. They are sixteen, "Dork Brains" he said, and are headed home, which is Silver Springs, Maryland, Lem ("Please call me Lem") is sure.

No, we can't help anyone, not him or ourselves, our own selves, I emphasize, thinking he might be slightly high on something, definitely on something if only his own adrenalin. It was at this point that Pat and Bess rescue us, but now we are in a van, one that is "loaded" as Angela says about her dream car, and we have this Lem person who is swept up in what should have been our rescue, just ours, not his.

Now I know that Bess and Pat's reasons for hanging out at bus stations and rescuing girls and this time a boy may spring from a religious impulse or something. I can't think of any other reasons. Suffice it to say, as Angela says, we left the bus station with them. The policeman looking relieved, we went out for steaks and baked potatoes at two-twenty in the morning with Lem, Bess and Pat. Lee Ann got right into their van which had everything, a deluxe beyond deluxe. I didn't know restaurants stayed open that late. As much as I have learned, I still have a long way to go. Lee Ann wanted tacos, but I persuaded her that steaks were nicer and that we could have tacos soon. Lem is a vegetarian, wouldn't you know, and had a baked potato with cheese and broccoli which he apologized for by saying he loved cliché foods.

One reason I'm agreeing for us to stay overnight again here with them, if I count last night as spending the night when it was not really a whole night because we did not get here until almost four—one reason out of seven or eight good ones—is that they keep telling Utah stories which, of course, I love, because they remind me of my blood Mama. And having Lem along, out of nowhere, has added a layer of confusion to our situation which I am trying to take advantage of, but am not sure exactly how to.

Bess and Pat don't know that they have hit my heart, my soft spot, with their stories, and as I said, they think I am learning about the dark side of Utah and so will want to go back to Virginia. Wrong. Not happening. Texas and Aunt Helen, they are not dealing with directly, but I saw Pat get out a pair of cowgirl boots from the top of her closet. Beautiful ones, and that told me everything I needed to know. Her heart is in the right place even if I can't get her to take us to Houston. Lem is making me want to visit Silver Springs too. In fact, he has invited me and Angela up for a weekend, which is as likely a thing to happen as saving the rain forests that he talks about all the time.

Pat makes Utah people sound dumb. She and Bess think they are making fun of Utah people, but the more they talk and tell their story of a baby being sacrificed on a dining room table because an angel named Macaroni, or something close to that, said to send the baby up to him, the more I realize that Utah is the place for us.

There's very little sex in Utah, they say, and that suits me fine. I guess they thought a pre-teen and teen would not be interested in a place without sex, but what I have seen about sex lives and what Angela has told me she has seen at the lake and cleaning up after people make me sick. Angela has planned her sex life and I will plan mine next year. She has set seventeen as the last year she will be a virgin. After that, she will find a suitable boy, one who is right for her at that time of her life: college-bound, varsity in one sport, occasional honor roll, not a natural reader because her

173

father is and she is afraid of men who depend on books for fun, not a church person, an appreciator of the Dead and hater of Van Halen, tolerant of the Eagles, conversant with political issues. I am quoting her list. Where is such a boy I want to ask, but I know her answer—right in front of us. She just needs to pick one we already know and then bring him out, develop his taste. Lem with a lot of tutoring and good food may apply for the position of Angela's boyfriend. He has said he is available.

Anyway, a couple of Bess's stories were about how the teenagers in Utah do not have sex. So where did the baby who was killed on the table come from, I wanted to ask, but Bess and Pat were laughing so hard at how one girl would only talk to her boyfriends through the locked door. I didn't think that was so funny or anything considering all the trouble sex has brought to Virginians and my family in particular. I notice that Lem was not laughing at that story either which made him go up in my estimation.

I would like for Lee Ann and me to live in a nice place like Utah, not a place where the first thought anyone has is naked people and rubbing legs and sneaking off and running off with other people's wives. Keith Peller is a good example of a Virginian with sex on the brain, Jeannine is another one. I have not tried to tell any of my stories to Pat and Bess or to Lem. What I know is too long for human conversation. Definitely book material.

Anyway, Lee Ann and I would make excellent citizens of Utah. We would like the stories of gold tablets and Jesus going to South America and Mr.

174

Smith finding gold books and black people dipped in bleach, but not the ones who helped Uncle David change a tire, just before they get to the pearly gates. We would like storing up food underground for emergencies like the end of the world. And best of all, we would love the beautiful music and my beautiful real mother singing in the Tabernacle. Pat described the pictures painted on the wall and they sound beautiful too. Great big Jesuses, great big children around him. Lem has said he would love to see Salt Lake.

I wish people in Virginia acted fast when an angel spoke, not kill a baby, of course, even if an angel did say to do it, but other things. I think I would fit in with people who heard what should be done and did it, post haste, as Mama would say. I do have good judgment, so I certainly would yell NO at any angel who gave such a stupid order, but if he gave a good one, like "GO LIVE WITH YOUR BLOOD MAMA" I would in a minute, as soon as I could find her in the telephone book or practicing with the Tabernacle Choir. Her last address was from a little place outside Salt Lake.

North Carolina (not Texas) will have to do for this summer. Utah is rising in my heart for next summer. It's funny what happens to a girl's dreams. My dreams do not die—I have to say that for them—but they do change. Now I'm planning to get to Utah next summer. I can never include Angela in my plans because she cannot leave her parents "to their own devices." She is their voice of reason, their guardian angel, hence her name, she says. They would be in

Chapter 11 or debtors' prison if she had not stopped them from all the deals they had lined up to develop the lake. The latest one was to start a regatta. I did not know that word until Angela told me its definition. Then we had a good, sad laugh. In the middle of nowhere, in the piedmont, the hinterlands as Mama would say, a regatta! In a place where people raise chickens, a regatta! I have told Lem some of Angela's life story, and he has fallen for her already.

I told him how Angela made the regatta joke even sadder and funnier by saying a regatta demanded by its very nature people who had grown up going to sailing camps and learning how to tie ropes in a cold, blowing salty spray while being dashed, or almost, on the rocks in Maine or Massachusetts. People needed white trousers and un-Southern accents. They could not value canning or the art of making light bread, or vegetable gardens, even mushroom farmettes like the one Uncle David wanted.

No, a regatta needed a different kind of population, not to mention a different kind of lake that was not so warm and coated with algae where you can see the snapping turtles' heads sticking up like little black triangles. Lem agreed with Angela on every point.

I will say that Angela Marks has parents who listen to her. They respect her judgment, a quality mine lack, and one that keeps Angela at home. She has no need in her heart to take off for Texas or Utah. She appreciates being respected and is committed—her word—to saving her parents from themselves. She compares her feelings for them to mine for Lee Ann. We are preventing disasters.

My English teacher is always saying nothing "broadens" like travel and I agree. Lem has been on school trips to Sea World, Madrid and Paris. He said his school was mainly for rich people who could organize trips almost anywhere they could persuade a teacher to go.

I am going to make a list of what I have learned from this trip while I wait to hear what Bess and Pat decide. They enjoy fighting, so it will take some time. They have made up a couch in their basement with the world's cleanest and best-smelling sheets, and I am staying awake only because I have some Baby Ruths and Zero bars stashed In my backpack.

When I am older, I will drink coffee, but until then, it's Baby Ruths. Lem is partial to Heath Bars which makes him a member of Angela's team, not mine.

Maybe I can start being a pen pal to Bess and Pat and over the year persuade them in letters to drive Lee Ann and me out to Utah. They could go collect more Utah stories to laugh at for another year and Lee Ann and I could go for serious reasons.

I'll get Mama and Walter to invite Pat and Bess to Virginia for a weekend, and Lem too. Who knows, Bess and Pat might enjoy driving their van around and looking at the farm houses and mills where Robert E. Lee slept after he surrendered. Some people do.

Lem is a Civil War nut, only he says "buff," and wants to see High Bridge that was burned by I forget which side just before the last battle. He figures it is near us, maybe fifty or so miles away.

The van is as nice as their house, with TV's and computers all built into the walls and sheepskin rugs on the floor, dark glass windows, a stove and refrigerator. Not the kind of camper I have ever seen, even in Walter's catalogs.

Lee Ann keeps as close to Pat as she can because Pat has the same shape as Mama, soft and damp and friendly.

Plus, Pat is a talker and Lee Ann can feel her big brown voice vibrating through her nice soft arms and I know it reminds her of home. Bess is as dark as Walter, but I don't see any other likeness.

Lee Ann puts her head on Pat's shoulder who just smiles. She is basically a stranger to us, and I can tell that she thinks she saved our lives by finding us in the bus station. I would not go that far. Pat can tell, but who couldn't, that Lee Ann doesn't know what she's doing exactly and that I'm the one in charge. In other words, I have to watch Pat because she is on alert about me. She is a kind person, they both are, especially with kids and with handicaps like Sis and runaways like Lem who has it written all over him. Lee Ann and I are harder to read. It is not often that a pair like us takes off in America. Pat and Bess are rare birds too, I know that.

First on my list of things I've learned from traveling is: MOST PEOPLE DON'T ACT RIGHT.

It's a relief to be around people who for some wonderful reason can see what they look at without twisting it up like a coat hanger to make a little design that suits them. The thing is that I am the one with the design and I am the one who needs to twist things around so that we keep on our way to Texas while Mama and Walter think we are at Camp Independence. I have to keep my goals clearly in my mind, but it is hard because I am so tired.

August 17

...This is what I'm hearing from Bess and Pat right now. They're fighting away in their bedroom over Lee Ann and me.

Bess says, "Texas, damn it, Pat."

And then Pat says in a voice made of stone, "You just want to go to Texas, yourself. It's certainly not to take those two back for a two-day visit to what the skinny one sometimes calls their "real home" and "to check on their Aunt Helen.""

Then there's a quiet time. Bess and Pat stopped arguing for a while. Then, Lee Ann started thrashing and soon we were lying on a real waterbed, king-size, with Bess and Pat running to get us Cokes. Pat opened her cigarettes. The noises of the crinkling cellophane on top of the sound of the water washing up against the sides of the bed seem to calm Lee Ann and the two of them down. It was a good thirty minutes before they were at it again about Texas or Virginia or Silver Springs which they can go to after they get us home.

I couldn't tell if Bess would win and we'd end up in Texas or if Pat's plan for Virginia (and Maryland)—one she would not come out and say because she has had training with runaways which she let slip and knows that any talk of going home is a no-no big time—would "triumph." That's a nice word we used in history class a lot and it fits here.

Pat seems a little bit smarter about people than Bess to me. Listening to them start up again, I have to give Pat an "A-" for seeing how I operate. I hear her saying I "manipulate" and she's got that right. She is almost yelling.

"That little Indian-looking thing can manipulate that poor epileptic woman-child into having those seizures. Don't you see that, Bess, you idiot?" Then she comes in to where we are and starts working on us and gets me to wake up completely, though I was not asleep really, of course. Pat says standing over me, "She's dead asleep." She is whispering and hissing, "We drive them to Texas where Crystal says she has people waiting for her, or we drive them to Virginia back to the people who let them run away. Our little game of catching runaways, our little do-good game at bus stations has hit a snag with this charmer, Ms. Crystal Ball. Oh, I forget, she has said we can drive them to Utah and find her beautiful "blood mama" and listen to The Choir. The whole thing is a plan of this string-bean girl. I saw her chopping up her sister's pills, so she can overdose, under dose, keep her straight or set her to 'thrashing.' We're her audience. If you can't see it, you're as stupid as you're blind. Mr. Lemuel What's His Name Craigleather is a regular suburban/entitled type of misfit. Unhappy with all the advantages, so off he goes on a road trip, joy ride and gets himself dropped off and left, or claiming he was left, at a gas station exit on route 85. He's lucky we got him, lucky as lucky can be."

"Pat, you're the one who's both blind and stupid. Don't you see, Crystal is losing control of her plan?

181

She's losing steam and can't you see why—she's exhausted from her trip. Just the few stories she told us, if they're half true, would kill an army. I don't want to go to Texas, certainly not take them. I do want us to help, really help this weird duo we've dragged home this time. These two have to be our Academy Award Winners; they take the cake. From what I was hearing, I thought Virginia was a dangerous place for these two. As Crystal was falling asleep, she went on and on about a Pellman or somebody, who was "hurting Sis." Then she'd almost cry about an Uncle David and his mean kids. She didn't know she was talking or that I was listening. That's why I say Texas, but I'll go to Virginia tomorrow if you really think it's best for our Crystal Ball and Lee Ann. Lem Weatherface is an easier problem a few phone calls can fix."

Then it was very, very quiet. They came around to Texas again, so I felt free to drift a little. Boy, I felt like I've gotten a free trip to a shrink. Bess and Pat had my number and almost understood our whole situation. Of course, they're mixed up a little from not knowing everything. Talking in my sleep, (right, believe that and you are retarded) I must have been feeding them strategic information that tore them up about what would be best to do.

I feel much, much older. And pretty much wiser, in some ways, anyway. "Camp Independence" is almost over. Pat and Bess are out in the driveway loading up the van with enough good food, chips, coolers, wet ones, foam mattresses, the works, to last us on the trip to Texas which won finally. I convinced them to go to Houston with the address of Mama's rental property and a long story about Aunt Helen living there on Locust Avenue which is true every word of it. There was no phone there yet, I improvised, because of the renovations going on. I went on about gentrification (thank you, Angela Marks, again, for a big word) in Houston and funding for housing in declining neighborhoods. They have bought the whole story.

I can't wait to hit the open road in their fantastic van that floats, not roars like the bus. I bet it does, I mean. From sitting in it and pretending to be sailing down the interstate, I think I know what it feels like. I won't have to pretend long.

They are walking around Lee Ann who's got it in her head we're going back home to Mama and Walter, so I avoid all discussions or picturing of travel or destination. It's best.

She has looked so sad and kept squeezing her arms around her shoulders that I had to act out one time all about home: Walter: acting big and quiet except when he's mad, and then Mama on one of her talk-a-thons. That's when Lee Ann understood the fact that the van was taking us home to them, so she crawled in it and won't come out. I overdid it, but couldn't stop myself. There's no particular reason she has to come out of the van with a bathroom just our size in the back. I hated to lie to her, but I had to. So, we're going to Texas, but Lee Ann is convinced and therefore, happy, that we're going to Virginia.

Pat and Bess are happy, they say, to see her so happy. I don't think they follow all the picturing I have been doing about home. What about me, my happiness, I want to ask, but I'm not sure I want to go

183

into detail about the ways and the whys I feel like Virginia is not as good as Texas for us right now. We will be back in Virginia soon enough, before school starts for sure. We are just on a vacation unless we do find a home away from home—for a few years anyway—while Mama and Walter get Uncle David's boys tamed down so we can stand it.

August 18

...It does float, I mean we are floating now, along Route 85. Texas bound. I have been trying to sleep only in spurts which is very hard to do. When we get off on the little side roads which Bess and Pat like better than interstate, we are going to stop at all the festivals—Pork, Cantaloupe, Peanut—along the way. I thought we'd stop at the outlets, but Pat and Bess are definitely festival, not outlet types. They want to do educational stuff and they mean well, but pork, peanuts and cantaloupe won't have a whole lot to teach me. I won't tell them, they're too good and sweet in their way, to hear that I think homemade festivals like those—No, I have not been to any except the Shrimp Festival and that was sickening—are a crock, as Keith Peller would say.

I am sorry I had a thought about Keith Peller except that it makes me glad we are headed toward Texas, away from him and Jeannine, Uncle David's not being there, Ms. Karney and all the messy sad stuff I left home to get away from. I hope being away for a while, "at camp," will give me energy, will make me strong enough to live the life I will have to live at home when we return "in triumph," a phrase I love from World History class. I am sure things are worse at home now, if that's possible. Uncle David's boys are there by now,

I guess, and I'll have to deal with them: protect all living things—like me, like Lee Ann.

Still, we are making a point and safe because Mama thinks we are at Camp, and we're only driving to Texas, staying two nights and turning around to drive back. It's crazy, but Pat and Bess seem to thrive on adventure, and they are on vacation, they said. I know how they feel, so that is why the way they jumped at the chance of driving to Houston was not strange to me because I know that just the thought of Utah, just the thought has been enough to make me happy and strong on many occasions, and I didn't have to actually go there. Hearing the Utah stories made me sure that Utah is exactly where I am going to get to one day.

Lee Ann will grow up and get worse, so the doctors say. I will grow up and keep getting better. Stronger, smarter. And even if I do not always get where I start out for directly or without problems, I eventually get there and I am learning something. For example, going to Salisbury, North Carolina, showed me the truth about two places—Texas where I soon will be (two days at most), and Utah, which I now know I will live in when I am grown, until I die and until Lee Ann dies.

I have to stop thinking now because I am going to take a little rest listening to them about the first festival they want to stop at. Pork. Now, Utah would have an Angel Festival or a Gold Book Festival or a re-enactment of how Mr. Smith moved to Utah. It would be something "grand," I know that, not something plain like pork or peanuts. I use "grand" because Angela's dad loves it. He has told her who told me that

186

Diamond Jim Brady used to say "grand" as he "lolled" at Sarasota and watched the fireworks with his girlfriend, Lillian Russell. "Ain't it grand, Nell!" he would say, according to Mr. Marks, who loves to say these words for big occasions.

Pat and Bess were thrilled with the barbecue barrels lined up on Main Street. I slept through the Pork Festival. When they were driving along real slow looking for a place to park and talking about the smoky smell, I must have gone off. Lee Ann had her head out the window like a real pretty dog, and of course, she has gotten in all of her z's, so she was ready for a snow cone and barbeque. She has taken to Pat especially. Bess thinks I am writing book reports for my summer reading list as I am writing in my book. I told them I had done all the reading in June and just had to write the reports down in my composition book.

I tried to picture to Lee Ann the fact that if we went back home we couldn't go on meeting interesting people and doing fun things, waking up in strange places and eating in restaurants, but she couldn't take it all in. The thought-picture of Mama blanks out all the other pictures—Texas, Utah—but when she forgets about Mama, she's so thrilled with the new life I have found for us. But, I am so tired and the windows are dark so I miss road signs, but we are spending the night on some little fairground that is filling up with campers and vans. Bess wants to stay and hear the Statler Brothers play tonight. She says she can't think of a better way to begin our trip to Texas than to roll out some blankets by the big lake here and listen to some good picking and singing. Pat asked her

187

when she had gone country. She said just today after eating the supper of sliced, smoked tenderloin. She did pile up her plate.

It all seems movie-perfect. Little kids falling asleep in happy parents' arms, happy parents drinking beer and sticking with their little kids, not running off in the bushes, so to speak, the way Keith Peller and Jeannine did.

That smoky smell, the twangy music, and the huge bonfire they built on a hill to drive off mosquitoes made Lee Ann happy. The fire didn't work too good, we got eaten up on our ankles and wrists, but it did make a good helpful impression. I told Bess that to me Utah was God's Country, maybe I should not have gone so far, knowing how they feel, but the atmosphere was working on me and I had to tell at least one true thing.

When I said that, Bess started looking at Pat and saying real fierce, "Listen to this child, listen to this child."

Pat asked if the night-time scene there looked like a good job market for systems analysts and wondered if Texas might need some computer whizzes. I thought it might and was glad to think of having them as friends in Houston if we got to stay.

We have three Apples at my school, I told them, but I had never had a turn on them even though I am honor roll. They laughed and we all lay down and looked at the stars through the curls of smoke and listened to what Bess called real music.

August 19

...To Bess and Pat, it's a great time, going to these festivals. They entered the cantaloupe-eating contest this afternoon and won third and fourth places. They were sure they would have diarrhea all night, but they laughed at that too. I'll have to say this for them, when they start having fun, they really have fun and don't stop, regardless of the circumstances. I slept through that festival too.

However, they would have their laugh machines tested at home with Mama and Walter and those three—Davey Jr., Ernest and James Howard. I would love to see if they'd think things were so much fun with a houseful of kids nobody wants around. Mama and Walter want Lee Ann and me because we're different from the boys. Number One, Lee Ann is afflicted, and people like Mama and Walter always will love a person who needs them. They're that type. Number Two, they are used to having me around. When Mama is feeling good, she will say that I am interesting and I know how to listen to her. And they also depend on me to take charge of Lee Ann. Of course, I'd be dumb not to be afraid that all that will change with Uncle David's hellions living there. Plus, Mama and Walter may go off the deep end and think I ran away with Lee Ann if they hear about this little trip to Texas.

It's not that simple. This book, DEAD AND GONE, as it used to be called, and now is called LOCAL SPEED, has explained completely why I took Lee Ann away. I will try to list clearly the reasons I am going home after our visit to Texas. I am ashamed in my heart of every living one of them.

1. HAVE NO MONEY. Lee Ann would need pills, Tampax, food.

2. ONLY older girls get noticed (or hired in the first place) as workers. I know I could sit with old ladies or wash dishes or take care of pets, but Oh No, I'm a kid and no one will hire me.

3. MISERY is what I see in Lee Ann around all Mama-shaped and sounding women. I can't stand that, so...

4. EVEN if I go home, I can always leave again. As I have said before, I know now that it can be done, and I have two new friends who just may drive me to Utah if only to prove to me what a terrible place it is.

I will now make a list about going to Utah. So I will spell-think out UNTIL I get to Utah.

1. UNTIL I am 16 at least, I have to wait at home in Virginia. The thought of the trip to Texas instead of the actual trip will be "sustaining," as Angela would say.

2. NO, I can't go where I want to yet. This is a fact.

3. TELLING my heart's story to this little notebook has helped me a lot.

4. I am happy in a new kind of way because I have taken "arms against a sea of trouble," as Angela's father would say.

5. LOVE does make the world go round, as the song is saying on the tape. I know that, though I do not understand it or how L learned it. The L word is Lemuel who may be Angela's and my friend. We will have to see how he works out.

August 19

...I must record the fact of Pat and Bess's treachery because we almost were killed because of it: We came home! We did not drive toward Texas. We, Lee Ann and I and Lemuel, are here, along with Bess and Pat, and I am able to write in my book, a miracle, because I haven't been to bed, to really go to sleep in, since we left Trooper Harris' in Danville, and that has been how many days ago? Three, at least.

I did fall asleep, into a coma actually, in the van after one of the festivals, and that allowed what happened to happen. Just as I thought we were finally on the road to Texas, the boots packed, on a free ride, the Houston tickets as good as cash for Utah when I would turn them in, driving along in the dark, not stopping at every little hoe-downing festival on the way out of North Carolina, we end up back in Virginia. It was stranger and faster and more dangerous than even I could have expected, though without the speed and danger, things would not have worked out as well as they have. Never discount bad things is a lesson I must remember.

It wasn't just the fact that I was sleeping; it was the fact that we ran into a storm that I have heard about since, had tornado watches on the radio, so even if I had been able to stay awake, I could not have told if we were heading to Texas or Virginia or the North

Pole. Just before I fell into that sleep that allowed the deception to take place, I saw that the rain drops were not normal tear-shaped drops, but long, round aluminum nozzles of water, shooting straight down from the sky. The lightning was splitting the black sky wide open like crazy and running along the electric wires, sizzling and catching fire like fat meat in a pan.

But, guess who went to sleep in the middle of the racket, stretched out in the bed in the back of the van. Only because Pat had to stop, and I felt it the different kind of movement, a still lurching and swaying in place, did I wake up. The noise of the storm was a high roaring, the wind coming down the interstate rocking the van like a cup in a saucer. It sounded like several packs of wolves were making a circle around the stalled van.

I looked out. What could I see? We were parked on the edge of a black hole! Pat had pulled off on the shoulder of the interstate (which I still thought was headed toward Texas) to wait for the rain to let up, but that was more dangerous, I heard Pat saying, because the hills that rose up from the highway had sheets of drink cans and trash riding down on layers of water into the creeks which were rising and running across the highways and alongside in the wide ditches. She had seen the water sluicing down the hills in a flash of lightning. I had never heard the word "sluicing" but I knew what it meant. I couldn't see anything, but took her word for how bad it was. Then, she and Bess decided it was better to creep along the highway than to park, but we were the only ones who thought so. We were the only ones driving if you can call going twelve miles per hour driving. Six hours we crept and stopped, stopped and crept. Twice the engine died. I fell back into my coma. Lee Ann was in one too because of the pills I had given her for the trip.

About twenty miles from home, I understood, even in the dark and the storm. In the pitch dark, I knew that the way to Texas was smoother and straighter than the roads we were on. I could feel the old bumps in the road, the old banked curves that approach our river.

There was nothing to say, and by then, I had had just enough rest to think fast.

When we rolled in no dogs barked. The dogs were scared witless and were tied up in knots under the porch. No lights went on. There was no electricity, and wouldn't be any for three days. Trees were down all along the road. The woods looked as if God had given them a haircut, stripped the leaves and all the limbs he wanted to off and tossed them all over.

I had a flash of hope that no one was at home, that something had called them away—a mass funeral for Davey Jr., Ernest and James Howard, and then the storm had kept them away.

No such luck. Still, a certain kind of violent luck was on my side.

So we are creeping and lunging up the driveway. Pat can't drive on rutted roads, only those people who grow up with them know how to keep the wheels lined up on the highest part of the ruts. I have had maybe twenty minutes preparation time to realize what was happening and how it did happen. Bess and Pat had driven north, not southwest toward Houston, so I

194

immediately try to jump out of the van, but the wind is so heavy and that aluminum rain is cutting me and thrashing me so bad that I jump back in the van and I bring on Lee Ann's attack of thrashing. Whole pill and a half slipped to her in Zeros, which are better for pills than Baby Ruths, at the Willis River Bridge.

She was twitching pretty good by the time we got to the mailbox, so I had all the way down our horrible, rutty road to get her going in high gear. It was going to be grander thrashing than we had seen at Danville with Trooper Harris. And she was going strong by the time the lights come on and Walter was yelling "Someone's here. Give me the flashlight!" I could have told him if I could have run the thirty steps to the house from the van that the flashlight was up with Ernest. He has to have one at all times with him, one or two. Mean as he is, he is afraid of the dark, but also afraid to admit it, so he steals matches and flashlights first thing when he comes to your house.

I could see the dogs getting up, not in circles like they do when nothing's happening, but straight up and barking before they completely woke up. It was surprise time. Then, just as I expected, out the upstairs window, the boys came sliding down the porch roof, then slid a little but mainly jumped from the corner of the roof to the ground. Lee Ann was on the ground scrounging around and around, and the thought did cross my mind that I had given her too much medicine, that I had killed her, and was watching her die in front of my eyes and also giving Mama and Walter another terrible tragedy to ruin what was left of their lives. They would have a dead Lee Ann and a murderer

Crystal Ball. They would not be able to think of Uncle David anymore. His death would reduce itself to a simple suicide.

Just to take the heat off me, to save my own skin, I fainted which was not too hard to do.

Lee Ann was spitting and gagging and I recovered from my faint to run to get the wooden spoon that keeps her tongue from rolling up in a knot and choking her. It was hanging with the truck keys right where I left it over the stove.

I ran quick as anything back out to Mama and handed her the spoon. She had Sis's head between her knees and Walter was holding her legs out straight. It was like old times, except there were five extra people looking on—two with horror written all over them, and the three boys with happiness scrawled all over them like graffiti. They were pointing and whispering, "A real crazy person," over and over.

Then Lee Ann went limp as a sock and that scared me nearly to death. "Call the rescue squad!" Mama was yelling over her shoulder to me.

I ran back in the house with Pat and Bess right behind me. They didn't know where anything was, much less the phone, but when I got the lights on, which, miracle of miracle, were back on, and then Bess did the dialing and talking. She said the right things without ever having been to our house in the woods before. I was amazed.

She knew the route number and the mailbox number.

It wasn't ten minutes before the red lights were coming up the hill. They know us all from the thing with Uncle David last summer, and who knows how many times his boys have fallen off the roof and had to be carried to the emergency room in the little time while we were gone, though they didn't, none of them, have on casts.

They loaded Lee Ann in the white rescue truck and took off. It was a team I didn't know, and they worked like real doctors. Then Bess yelled at all of us standing there to jump in the van and we took off like bats out of hell for Richmond, right behind the rescue wagon.

Lee Ann did not die. I did not either, but I wished I could have died many times last night on the drive in and as we sat in the room they call the Family Room while the doctors worked on her. Pumping her stomach did the trick, they said. I could have used a blood transfusion by the time they came out to tell us she was okay. They said her system was overloaded, not just with the medicine, but by the stress of being in a "new environment." Rest should fix her up. They wanted her medicine monitored more carefully. Camp was a good idea, the doctors said, if the medicine intake could be measured more carefully.

Mama and Walter had pulled on their clothes so fast that they looked worse than usual, Mama with her hair flat in the back and puffing up high in the front. To me, though, she looked beautiful. I introduced them to Bess and Pat and they seemed to skip over the getting-to-know-you part of friendship and jumped right to the best friends' part. I guess it was the close call and the ride to the hospital behind Lee Ann.

No one, not even Mama, blamed me for almost killing Lee Ann. I will have to live with this in my heart all my life now, but I honestly think it is better to carry it in my heart than to tell Mama and Walter who would surely, or might anyway, kill me, and then there would be another trip to try to save me after they saw me limp on the ground like Lee Ann was last night. I know they'd regret it when they saw me half dead and would call the rescue people again.

So, I'm putting the truth in this book along with the truth as I see it about Uncle David. He was killed—in a way—by Keith Peller who evidently thought one crime was not enough and that he had some left over fun left for himself with Lee Ann. Sometimes I think that I—in a way—almost killed my sister. I am not like Keith Peller, but the truth is very hard to understand if you just look at the facts. And I have written down the facts, but I can see they are not as clear as I had hoped they'd be when I started this book. As Mama would say about this situation, "Alas."

Bess and Pat are still asleep out in the van. Mama and Walter think that they are somehow connected to Camp Independence, that they brought us home because we were so homesick, which is true when you think about it loosely.

The boys are playing quiet as mice in the dirt by its back wheels. I think the big Waffle House breakfast Pat treated us all to on the way home this morning with Lee Ann resting in the van won them over, and they are treating Pat and Bess like long-lost fairy godmothers. They are circling around Lem, shocked to find a boy here, thrilled out of their minds. I lucked out there too: they think I am responsible for finding a boy and bringing him home to them. So, now the boys treat me like the adopted daughter of the two godmothers, a person who has brought them a present. They have a new attitude toward Lee Ann since they saw her almost die. Anyone who goes to the hospital to die, not just to get a bone set, has those boys under control. And, they respect crazy people which they think Lee Ann is.

Things could be much worse than they are. Camp Independence will be calling as soon as the phone is fixed, I won't lay out all the little details of how much worse things could be, but believe me, and I know they could be. I am working on what I will say when Pam Roper calls and how I will handle her. I have confidence in my ability and, if there is time, I may have Angela's help if I can get to her on the phone before I have to talk to Pam. Of course, there is Lem, who seems to know a little about a lot of things, and he won't be leaving for a day or two. "All may yet be well," as Mama used to love to say.

September 11

...RICHMOND---After a high-speed, thirty-five-mile chase through three counties, police forced a van with Lynchburg tags on it off Interstate 64. The van crashed into the bridge just east of the Short Pump exit and burned. It was driven by a man who evidently was abducting two girls from the Sandys Point area. The unidentified man was dead on arrival at Henrico Doctors Hospital. The girls who are in critical condition had been missing for three days. State Trooper Morgan Guthridge tried to stop the van in a routine D.U.I. traffic check because the van had been weaving across the lanes of the highway. When the driver ran through the check point, Trooper Guthridge pursued him, not knowing that the girls were in the back of the van. Evidence of drugs was found in the charred wreckage of the van. The man died on impact, not in the fire. Crystal Annette Ball and Lee Ann Ball, foster children of June and Walter Ball of Sandys Point are in the Intensive Care Unit at St. Mary's Hospital.

The diary of the younger girl was found a mile from the crash site. Trooper Guthridge had seen an object fly out of the van as he was giving chase to the vehicle. The court has ordered the family to allow it to be read as part of the investigation of the incident and in an effort to identify the driver of the van. The mother of the girls said that the younger girl wanted to write novels and that the diary was, in her opinion, probably entirely made up. She did not know that her foster daughter kept a diary. The family, the mother said, had been under a great deal of stress during the past year and that she did not have any idea of who the man might have been.

About the Author

Susan Pepper Robbins lives in rural Virginia with her husband, a writer. Her first novel was published when she was fifty ("One Way Home," Random House, 1993). Her fiction has won prizes (the Deep South Prize, the Virginia Prize) and has been published in journals. Her collection of stories "Nothing But The Weather" was published by the indie press Unsolicited Press, and her second novel, "There Is Nothing Strange," was published in England in 2016 by Holland House Books. A second collection of stories will be published by the indie press, Bowen Books. Her stories focus on the drama of ordinary lives. She teaches writing at Hampden-Sydney College.

www.ingramcontent.com/pod-product-compliance
Lightning Source LLC
Chambersburg PA
CBHW071434260626
47170CB00008B/2709